DEEP WATER

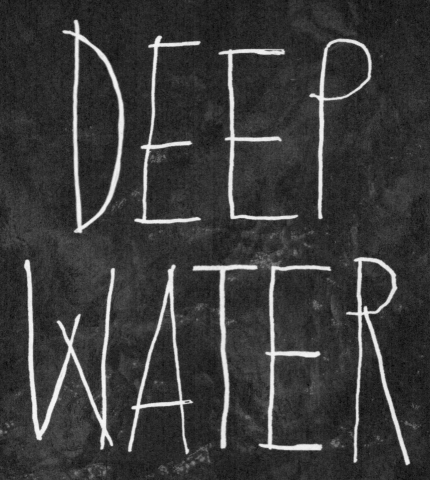

MAREN STOFFELS

TRANSLATED BY LAURA WATKINSON

DELACORTE PRESS

Delacorte Press
An imprint of Random House Children's Books
A division of Penguin Random House LLC
1745 Broadway, New York, NY 10019

penguinrandomhouse.com
GetUnderlined.com

Text copyright © 2023 by Maren Stoffels
Cover photo copyright © 2025 by Neil Holden/Arcangel
Translation copyright © 2025 by Laura Watkinson

Penguin Random House values and supports copyright. Copyright fuels creativity, encourages diverse voices, promotes free speech, and creates a vibrant culture. Thank you for buying an authorized edition of this book and for complying with copyright laws by not reproducing, scanning, or distributing any part of it in any form without permission. You are supporting writers and allowing Penguin Random House to continue to publish books for every reader. Please note that no part of this book may be used or reproduced in any manner for the purpose of training artificial intelligence technologies or systems.

Delacorte Press is a registered trademark and
the colophon is a trademark of Penguin Random House LLC.

Editor: Alison Romig
Cover Designer: Casey Moses
Interior Designer: Kenneth Crossland
Production Editor: Colleen Fellingham
Managing Editor: Tamar Schwartz
Production Manager: Liz Sutton

Library of Congress Cataloging-in-Publication Data is available upon request.
ISBN 978-0-593-90055-0 (trade)—ISBN 978-0-593-90056-7 (ebook)

The text of this book is set in 12-point Scala Pro.

Manufactured in the United States of America
1st Printing

The authorized representative in the EU for product safety and compliance is Penguin Random House Ireland, Morrison Chambers, 32 Nassau Street, Dublin D02 YH68, Ireland, https://eu-contact.penguin.ie.

Random House Children's Books supports the
First Amendment and celebrates the right to read.

For Joseph.
No matter how hopeless a situation might seem,
there's a way out. Thank you for your story.

&

For Noa.
You gave me a glimpse of your world.
Thank you for your trust.

&

For Maria.
Your strength is incredible.
Thank you for your honesty.

1. ON BOARD

VESPER

All around me, there's water.

Bright blue, as far as the eye can see.

I clutch the railing and stare back at the spot we came from. The harbor's no longer visible, and neither is Dad. When we said goodbye, he hugged me tight for the first time in ages, as if he didn't want to let go of me.

But he didn't say anything, not one word.

And I get that.

Being good at saying goodbye isn't in our genes.

But still, Dad let me go. In fact, he was the one who came up with the idea for this cruise. He says I need it.

When I heard the words "an amazing vacation for young people," I refused at first. But when Dad told me where the vacation was going to be, I was sold. Ten days on a cruise ship, with nothing around you but the sea. It sounded so tempting.

"How on earth did we afford this?" I asked Dad when I saw the ship. It was the kind of thing you see in brochures: white and gleaming, even more beautiful than I'd hoped. And so big! Plenty of floors to get lost on.

But Dad didn't answer my question.

I just hope he hasn't started gambling again.

One day, he's going to gamble away our house.

Or Ollie.

There must be lots of people out there who'd like to have a beautiful chocolate Labrador like Ollie. I think about his soft ears, which I held to my cheek just before leaving. Dogs aren't allowed on board, but I really wish I could have smuggled him onto the ship in my backpack.

I pick at the railing. The paint flakes off. As a sharp piece lodges under my fingernail, I wince.

"Welcome aboard this Dean Sea Lines cruise," a man's voice calls through a loudspeaker. "We hope you have a wonderful time with us. And our staff would love to give you a personal welcome on Foredeck A. Be there in five minutes."

I suck the sharp flake of paint from under my fingernail and spit it out into the sea. The pain throbs and then fades.

"That all you've got?"

When I look around, I see someone with such bright orange hair that it hurts my eyes. In fact, everything about him hurts my eyes, from that hair to his white T-shirt with three red stripes on the sleeves. His checkered pants don't go with the look—they're like something from a different century.

"I'll show you how to spit into the sea." He grabs the railing with both hands, leans back, gives a big sniff, and then swings forward in one fast movement.

The blob of spit flies through the air.

"That's how you do it."

"Charming." I turn around and lean on the railing.

"Why don't you put your backpack down? That thing looks heavy."

"Nah, I'm good," I say quickly. He'd better not ask what's in it. . . .

"Looking forward to our little vacation?" he says, turning his back to the sea as well.

"Yeah."

"So, who wanted to get rid of you?"

Huh? No one wants to get rid of me.

"With me, it was both of my parents. They kept nagging me until I said I'd go."

"My dad wanted me to do it," I say. "Because I . . ."

Because I need a rest, I think, but I don't say it.

"What about your mom?"

"My mom's dead." I hate saying those words out loud, but it's something I have to do pretty often. Ever since she died, it's like every conversation leads to her, as if people can *smell* it.

"That's a bummer."

Did he actually just say that? A *bummer* is when you get a failing grade, even though you studied really hard. Or when you forgot to grab a towel and you're dripping in the shower.

A dead mom is way more than "a bummer."

"So, it was your dad who signed you up?"

I look at him. "For a cruise, yeah. You're acting like this is some kind of hellhole!"

He smiles. "Guess we'll find out soon enough."

"Well, it doesn't look much like a hellhole." I gaze up at the huge white ship. "There's a movie theater, a pool, a library, a . . ." I swallow the word *casino*. "So, not very hellish."

"Oh yeah, it's incredible." He's still smiling. "Almost too good to be true."

He's crazy. I should have known. No normal person would dress like that. How did I manage to attract such a weirdo already? Bet I won't shake him off for the rest of the vacation.

"We have thirty seconds left." He taps his watch. "Then they're going to come fetch us for the welcome talk."

"I don't want to go." I can't bear that kind of thing. I

hate standing around in a group while someone gives a speech. It reminds me of school.

"Don't think you're getting out of it." He looks at me. His eyes are the color of a latte macchiato, Mom's favorite drink. Not mine, though. Way too much milk. You can hardly even call it coffee.

"No, I'm not going," I say. "If I don't want to do something, then I don't do it."

He bursts out laughing. "They must love you at school."

I don't reply. If he knew what's been going on at school lately . . .

"Ten more seconds," he says. "And five, four, three, two . . ."

"No one's coming," I say as he finishes the countdown. "See? No one cares if we're there or not."

"Oh, I think they do." He keeps looking around.

I look back at the sea. Hopefully this guy is going to beat it soon, or I'll just have to go in search of a quiet place to hide by myself.

"Hey, Jonah! Vesper!" someone shouts. A platinum blond in a white pantsuit with gold buttons comes striding across the deck.

"Here they come," whispers the boy standing beside me, who's apparently called Jonah. Has this woman somehow memorized everyone's names? Not bad. When Dad and I were saying goodbye, I saw loads of kids boarding the ship.

"We missed you guys."

Missed us?

"Just as I predicted." Jonah looks at his watch and smiles again. "You're right on time."

The woman smiles back at him. "So, are you coming?"

"Welcome on board this Dean Sea Lines cruise. My name's Tina, and I'll be your host."

The woman who came to fetch Jonah and me is standing in front of us on the outside deck, on the third step of the staircase. There's a big group, about sixty of us. We're all around the same age, but no one seems to know anyone else, because no one's talking.

"Before the vacation kicks off, I have a few announcements to make."

Everyone sighs.

Maybe I can sneak away now?

I turn around, but there's a man in an orange shirt standing behind me. He has a scar across his cheek, and his eyes are small and piggy.

"This isn't going to take long, Vesper."

How does he know my name? Who is this guy?

Something about his voice and the way he's standing makes me stay where I am. With a sigh, I look forward again, pulling the straps of my backpack a little tighter. My back's sweaty, but there's no way I'm taking it off.

"There are folders in your cabins with all the information about your stay. Go take a look at it. You're free to make use of all the facilities, but we expect everyone to be in their cabins by ten p.m."

Loud boos come from the crowd.

"That's bullshit!" one guy yells. His hair is shaved at the sides, with long bangs over his eyes.

"Breakfast is at seven-thirty a.m., lunch is around twelve-thirty, and dinner is at seven. The plan is that we'll come together to eat all our meals."

I sigh. *Together.* Why is that necessary?

"What about drink?" the guy shouts.

"What do you mean?"

"You know . . . ," he says with a grin. "Booze cruise!"

"Alcohol is off-limits for the ten days of the cruise," says Tina, looking at him sternly. "I'm sorry, but we promised your parents."

Parent, I correct her in my head.

I picture Dad, with Ollie sitting at his feet. Are they missing me yet? Ollie is, for sure. Dad's laps of the neighborhood are no match for my long walks on the beach.

"Is everything clear?" Tina asks. "Then have a fun first day! Go check out your cabins, everyone."

The group starts moving.

"What's your room number?" someone says.

"Eight," yells the guy with the long bangs. "So, which pretty lady would like to share with Jumper?"

A few of the girls giggle. Is he seriously called Jumper, or is that just his nickname?

"The allocation of the cabins is fixed," shouts Tina. "There'll be no moving around!"

"Too bad." Jumper gives one of the girls a grin.

I take an envelope out of my pocket. It contains a welcome letter and my key card. Cabin number 25.

Stuffing the envelope back into my pocket, I head in the opposite direction. Now that everyone's off to their cabins, I'm free to explore the ship.

"Vesper?" I feel a hand on my arm. The man with the piggy eyes is staring at me. "Where are you going?"

"Um . . . to the top deck?"

"Is there a problem, Harrold?" Tina says, walking over to us.

The man in the orange shirt lets go of me. "She wants to go up top."

Tina shakes her head. "No, no, sweetheart. Check out your cabin first."

Sweetheart. That word makes my skin crawl.

"Why?" I ask.

"I already told you. You need to read the information folder first." She nods at Jonah, who's already heading for the cabins. "Believe me, you'll have all the time you need to explore the ship after that."

When I insert the key card into the slot, the light turns green. The door slides open, and I step inside.

The door automatically closes behind me.

When I see the cabin, I gasp. The white sheets on the bed, the table with the bottle of sparkling water on it, the huge screen on the wall, the red carpet on the floor—everything looks so luxurious.

My sneakers sink into the red plush.

It feels like I've just walked onto a movie set.

No—into a movie star's dressing room.

Am I seriously going to be allowed to sleep here for ten days?

I walk over to the large window, which has a view of the sea. The swaying of the ship on the waves makes me feel calm. It's like sitting in a massive rocking chair.

Suddenly I don't mind that Tina sent me to my room.

I take off my backpack and put it down on the single bed. For a moment, I rest my hand on the front pocket, which is warm from the sun.

Has Dad realized yet that something's missing from home?

The information folder is on the bedside table. Do I really have to read it right away?

I'm sure Tina and Harrold won't notice if I take a dip in the pool instead. Better to do it now than in a few minutes, when everyone will be there.

I pull my swimsuit and a towel out of my backpack.

Then I walk back to the door and slip my card into the slot. But this time the door doesn't open.

Even when I rub the card on my jeans and try again, nothing happens.

The light stays red.

What's going on?

I look around. In hotels there's usually a telephone you can use to call the reception desk, but there's no sign of one here.

Instead, the screen on the wall suddenly comes to life, and I see a man's face.

"Hello."

The voice booms into the room, and I'm so shocked that I actually jump. Who the hell is he?

The man is wearing a white shirt and has dark hair, bushy eyebrows, and piercing eyes. He seems to be looking through the screen and straight at me.

"Welcome to No Exit."

What?

I look at the door, which is still closed.

No exit? Is this a joke?

"Welcome to No Exit," the man repeats. "The place for you so that others will be safe."

DIARY OF

He suddenly came and sat across from me at break time today. Started eating his sandwich, calm as anything, like it was completely normal for him to be sitting there.

As he chewed, he kept staring at me, like I was an animal in the zoo.

Chew.

Gulp.

Stare.

Chew.

Gulp.

Stare.

Made me really nervous.

Could he see ▓▓▓▓▓▓▓▓▓▓

He can't know about that. Can he?

When he'd finally finished his sandwich, he just smiled.

He stood up and walked away.

Reading this makes me so mad.
██████████████
██████████████████

People stare at me all day long.
Like they think ██████████████
I wish they'd make it illegal to stare at people.

VESPER

Even before I realize what the man said, the screen goes dark again.

Did he seriously say that other people would be safe without me?

Images flash by, and I immediately push them away. *Don't think about that now. None of this makes sense.*

There's no way that guy could know about all that.

He must be the ship's captain. At least, that's what he looked like.

I press a button on the screen, but nothing happens. All I see in the black screen is myself: shoulder-length dark hair, big eyes, pointed chin. I have Mom's face.

I walk back to the door and put my card back into the slot. It's no good. The light stays red.

Then I hear a short tune. The screen is back on!

I see a logo with orange letters. *NO EXIT* are the words

that appear on the screen. The letter O is a life buoy. A recorded voice repeats the words that the man just said: *"No Exit. The place for you so that others will be safe."*

What the hell is going on?

"I completely forgot to introduce myself." The man is on the screen again. "I'm Ted, your captain."

Seems I was right.

"Please read the information in your folders carefully and follow the instructions. You have an hour."

And the screen goes black again.

"No!"

At first, I think the scream came from Ted, but it's a different voice. It also sounds much closer, as if someone's in my room.

I turn around. And that's when I see the doorway next to the bathroom. There's no actual door, just a gaping hole.

Why didn't I notice it right away? I only had eyes for the beautiful view.

"Who's there?" I ask.

"No!" the voice shouts again.

I'm not going crazy. There really is someone there!

Cautiously, I walk to the doorway, and to my surprise, I see a room that's identical to mine. The same red carpet, the same white sheets, but sitting on the bed, there's . . . a girl.

She's staring ahead with big wide eyes. She looks so scared that it scares me too.

"Who . . . ," I manage to say. "Who are *you*?"

Why did no one say we'd have to share cabins?

The girl looks my way. "Th-this is a mistake."

"What's a mistake?"

"This!" the girl screams. "I'm not supposed to be here!"

Why is she so hysterical? I take a step into her room.

"Just calm down. . . ."

"Calm down?" The girl's eyes dart in all directions. "Do you have any idea where we are?"

"On a ship," I say. "It's a vacation for young people."

The girl bursts out laughing, but she sounds anything but happy. "You really believe that?"

I remember what Ted said, his words echoing in my mind.

No Exit.

What did he mean?

"We're locked up here."

"Locked up?" I repeat. "Don't be dumb. Of course we're not."

The girl gropes around and grabs her phone. She presses a few buttons and waits.

"No reception." The color drains from her face. "Which is obviously why they let us hang on to these things."

"Calm down," I say again. "We just need to wait until

our key cards work again. There must be some kind of technical problem."

The girl laughs even louder. "Do you know what No Exit is?!"

"No," I say.

"It's a reeducation program."

Now it's my turn to burst out laughing. A reeducation program? This girl's not right in the head.

"That's right," the girl says. "For bullies."

I gasp for breath. It's like she just sent a bullet through me. Those images fill my head again, much more vividly now. I see The Girl in front of me, covered in tears and snot. She begged me to stop, but I didn't.

"What's your name?" I quickly ask, changing the subject.

"Gwen." She throws her phone back onto the bed. "I shouldn't be here. My mom and dad would never do this to me!"

"Your mom and dad?"

Gwen slams her fist on the bed. "How do you think I ended up here?"

Who wanted to get rid of you?

That was what Jonah asked me.

Gwen's the second person to mention parents.

I picture Dad, just before I came on board. Is that why he hugged me so tight? Because he knew what was in store for me?

Did Dad sign me up for this?!

No, he can't have.

A reeducation program for bullies—there's no such thing, is there?

Gwen is just messed up in the head, like Jonah. They're inventing stories.

Dad gave me a ten-day vacation—and that's all this is.

It's about time the door opened so I can finally go swimming. I'm here to relax and to forget about everything that happened in the past year, not to be spooked by a boy with questionable fashion sense and a girl with hysteria.

I'm just about to go back to my room when Gwen says, "So, are you a bully, then?"

I spin around and spit the words out. "Shut your—"

"I'm certainly not. This is all one big mistake. I shouldn't be here. I . . ." Gwen's eyes look watery. I hope she's not about to start blubbing.

But luckily, she blinks her tears away.

I return to my own part of the cabin and try my phone, but I see that she's right: there really is no reception here.

I try my key card again, but there's no point doing that either. The screen remains blank and silent.

No Exit, a reeducation program for bullies.

Why have I never heard of it?

Simple.

Because it doesn't exist.

This must be some kind of welcome game. Some activity vacations start with an icebreaker activity, like a scavenger hunt. This is just a bit more extreme.

Maybe this is an escape room and Gwen and I have to search for clues together.

Didn't Ted say we have an hour? You always get an hour in escape rooms too!

No Exit. It even *sounds* like an escape room.

I snatch the folder from the bedside table.

Let Gwen be all hysterical, and I'll get us out of here on my own. I did an escape room not so long ago, and I was out in less than forty-five minutes.

On the first sheet inside the folder, it says in big black letters: NO EXIT.

I can't help it—my whole body freezes.

I quickly read on.

WELCOME TO NO EXIT.
THE PLACE FOR YOU
SO THAT OTHERS WILL BE SAFE.

Bullying isn't illegal.

You might be called to the principal's office, and in the worst-case scenario you'll get suspended from school.

But locked up?

I've never heard of such a thing before. Not until now.

> NO EXIT IS A UNIQUE REEDUCATION PROGRAM FOR BULLIES.
> THE NEXT TEN DAYS WILL BE THE HARDEST TEN DAYS OF YOUR LIFE.
> WHAT IMPACT DO YOUR ACTIONS HAVE ON OTHER PEOPLE?
> DO YOU DARE TO CONFRONT YOUR OWN BEHAVIOR?
> THE PEOPLE AROUND YOU WANT YOU TO CHANGE.
> NOW IT'S YOUR TURN.

I drop the folder onto the bed.

Not because of what I just read, but because of what's written below.

> ERNST HERZOG HEREBY DECLARES THAT HE IS ENROLLING HIS DAUGHTER, VESPER HERZOG, IN THE NO EXIT PROGRAM.

I stare at the signature in blue ink.

It's Dad's writing.

It almost feels like the day Mom died.

She abandoned me, just like that, from one day to the next.

But this time it's my dad who's abandoned me.

"Dad . . . ," I whisper. "Why did you do it?"

"Do you believe me now?" Gwen is standing with one foot in my room, holding on to the doorframe.

This isn't an escape room. It's not even close.

A reeducation program for bullies. What kind of person comes up with an idea like that?

How did Dad know what was going on at school? I never told him anything about it, and since Mom died, he always seems to be sleepwalking.

He's never there, not really.

Did school call him? They must have. I sweep my hand over the signature, as if I could wipe it out, then turn to look at Gwen. "What should we do?"

"Read the information in the folder," she answers. "We have an hour. You heard that Ted guy."

"So you want to do what he says?"

I think about Ted's piercing eyes. Who is he? Who are the others on this ship?

That Tina is obviously part of it. And Harrold with his piggy little eyes, too.

Tina came to fetch Jonah and me because we had to be in our cabins in time. Jonah told me what was going to happen.

But how could he know?

"We need to cooperate," says Gwen. "I want to get out of here as soon as possible."

I look at the view again. There are no bars on the windows, but it suddenly feels like a prison. A luxury prison, but still a prison. No exit.

That other sentence echoes inside my head.

The next ten days will be the hardest ten days of your life.

What are they going to do?

What exactly does this reeducation program involve?

I look at my backpack. If Mom were still alive, I wouldn't have ended up here.

And everything would never have become such a mess.

"Will you read what it says in the folder for me?" Gwen asks. "Please?"

"Why?" I look at her. "Are you dyslexic or something?"

"No." Gwen says with a smile. For the first time, her eyes look a little less wide and panicky. "I'm blind."

DIARY OF

Today he said no one will ever dare to kiss me.
   That I'm a freak.
   That it's a shame I was ever born.

   If I could, I'd lock him up.
   Far away from the outside world.
   That might be even better than killing him. Then I'd have all the time and space I needed to do whatever I wanted to him.
   Does such a place exist?
   It has to.

VESPER

"You're blind?" I stare at Gwen's eyes. How come I didn't notice?

"Yeah." Gwen takes a few steps forward, finding the way to my bed. As soon as she's sitting, she takes a deep breath.

"It's only been five years, though."

"You say that like it's nothing."

"I'm used to it."

I think about Mom. Will I get "used to" her not being around when she's been dead for five years? Or will that never happen?

"Would you read what it says?"

I look at Dad's signature again and then quickly turn the page. "Sure."

EVERY MEAL WILL BE EATEN WITH THE REST OF
THE GROUP IN THE RESTAURANT ON DECK A.

> BREAKFAST IS AT 07:30.
> LUNCH IS AT 12:30.
> DINNER IS AT 19:00.
> IF YOU'RE LATE, NO FOOD.
> EVERYONE MUST BE IN THEIR CABIN BY 22:00.

I remember the group booing when Tina gave her little speech. There seemed to be just one strict rule back then, but now it's much more than that.

> NO CONTACT WITH HOME FOR TEN DAYS.
> YOU WILL WEAR YOUR UNIFORM AT ALL TIMES. THIS CAN BE FOUND IN YOUR CLOSET. NO UNIFORM = NO ACCESS TO THE SHIP BEYOND YOUR CABIN.
> ANY REBELLIOUS BEHAVIOR, ESCAPE ATTEMPTS, OR REFUSAL TO PARTICIPATE IN TASKS WILL RESULT IN SANCTIONS.
> ANY PROBLEMS, TALK TO TINA.

"Do you know who Tina is?" Gwen asks.

"She's the one who just spoke to us," I say. "That woman in the white . . . I mean, with the supersweet voice."

"I wasn't there for the welcome talk," says Gwen. "When I got here, I asked to be taken straight to my room. I wanted a bit of peace and quiet. Going on vacation with so many other people is kind of . . . intense for me."

"Why did you want to come in the first place, then?"

"Because my mom and dad thought it would be good for me." Gwen makes a face. "Being left to my own devices for ten days, being more independent." Her voice is trembling, as if she's about to burst into tears.

"Do you want me to read the rest?" I ask quickly.

Gwen nods. "Yes."

NO EXIT IS MADE UP OF TWO PHASES: KARMA AND CONFRONTATION.

"Karma? What do they mean?"

"It doesn't say." I turn the page, but there's nothing else in the folder. "That was everything."

It's suddenly so silent in the cabin. The only sound is the quiet hum of the air-conditioning.

"I shouldn't be here," Gwen says again. This time her eyes look *really* watery.

"Don't cry," I say.

"But I haven't done anything!" Gwen hits the bed.

"Don't cry," I repeat.

But Gwen's not listening to me. In fact, more tears well up in her eyes.

I take a step forward and grab hold of her wrists. "I mean it. STOP!"

Gwen's eyes dart back and forth. "What are you doing?"

"Listen to me." I squeeze a little harder. "You are going to stop crying *now*."

For a moment I think she's actually about to burst into tears, but then she nods slowly.

Her tears seem to retreat, like a scared animal going back into its hole.

Then, carefully, I let go of her. Her wrists are red where I was holding them. I stare at her skin for a moment before quickly turning around.

"You're right, what you just said," I say. "We need to get out of here as soon as possible, so we'll play along for now. I'll grab our uniforms."

"What do you think?" Gwen runs her hands over the fabric of her overalls.

The thought of looking exactly the same as her drives me crazy.

The uniforms are dark-blue overalls, like something a farmer would wear. Written on the back in big orange letters are the words *NO EXIT*. On the front of my uniform it says *25A*. Gwen has *25B* on hers.

"I can't wear this," I say. "They've given us numbers."

"We have to if we want to leave the cabin," says Gwen.

I know she's right, but I can't do it. This is inhumane.

Gwen holds out her arms. "It's exactly the right size."

I nod. "They know our sizes."

I have no idea how it's possible, but it's true. Did Dad give them my measurements? He must have.

Why did he do it?

He must have known exactly what happened at school. What I did to The Girl.

"What do you think the sanctions are?" asks Gwen.

"I don't want to find out. But I am going to go look for Jonah."

"Who's that?"

"Another"—the word *bully* sticks in my throat—"another participant. He seemed to know a lot about No Exit. I need to speak to him."

At that moment, we hear a loud voice outside.

"Bullies, step away from the door."

Gwen and I automatically step back and—finally!—the door slides open. I'm about to heave a sigh of relief, but then I see the man in front of us.

It's Harrold, in his orange shirt. His piggy little eyes are cold and distant.

He runs his eyes over our uniforms and gives a nod of approval.

"Twenty-Five A and Twenty-Five B. Come on."

He's calling us by our numbers.

I take a step forward, and Gwen follows me. I'm back in the corridor where I was an hour ago.

But back then I was still myself, looking forward to a vacation and some rest. And now I'm 25A, a number.

I've watched dozens of shows about life in prison. Documentaries about violent criminals behind bars, thrillers about inmates trying to escape, and even a series about a woman who fell in love with a fellow prisoner.

But it was never like it is now.

This isn't exciting. This isn't romantic.

This is a complete nightmare.

I look down the long corridor and see loads more dark-blue overalls coming out. Dozens of kids, all dressed exactly the same as Gwen and me.

Just like during the welcome talk, everyone is silent.

The girl from the cabin next to ours is called 24B, and she looks like she's about to burst into tears.

I quickly turn away.

And then I see that no one's standing to my right. Gwen and I are the last two in the corridor.

That means there are exactly fifty of us.

"Eight B!" A loud voice startles me. At the other end of the corridor, there's another guard, in an orange shirt just like Harrold's. There are three of them, I see now, and they're all carrying batons. "Eight B, step into the corridor."

Everyone looks at cabin number 8. The boy with the long bangs is standing outside the door. Jumper.

But apparently his cellmate is still inside.

What's going on with 8B? Who is it?

"Eight B, final warning." The guard yells so loud that the floor seems to shake.

And then he goes into the cabin.

A second later, he's back, and this time he's dragging 8B by the arm. A boy with hair that's a perfect match for the guard's orange shirt.

"It's Jonah," I say quietly to Gwen. "He's not wearing his uniform."

"Where is your uniform, Eight B?" the guard roars.

"At home," comes Jonah's answer. "I forgot to iron it, sir."

There's cautious laughter.

"Ah, a smart guy."

"I do my best." Jonah sounds so bright and cheerful that it's as if he completely missed Ted's briefing.

"Put your uniform on," the guard says.

"Dark blue doesn't suit me." Jonah points at his white T-shirt and checkered pants. "I never wear it."

"Put it on," the man repeats. "Now."

"Don't you have any other colors? Pink, maybe? Gold, if need be?"

What's he up to?

Harrold leaves me and Gwen and walks toward Jonah.

"Got us a joker, have we?" I hear him say. He sighs. "There's always a couple. Every year."

Harrold looks around at the group. "Every. Single. Year."

As he says that last word, he turns back to Jonah and lashes out with his fist. Jonah collapses and sinks to the ground, clutching his stomach.

The girl from cabin 9 winces and steps back. It feels like I'm frozen to the spot, like I'll never thaw again.

Now we know what the sanctions involve.

"Okay, Eight B." Harrold looks down at Jonah. "Put. Your. Uniform. On."

We're standing in long lines on Deck A. There are now ten guards in orange and they're keeping a close eye on us.

I don't think that's necessary, because no one's moving.

After that punch to Jonah's stomach, something changed. It's like I suddenly woke up.

When I saw Dad's signature, I realized that No Exit really exists, but after Jonah was punished, I understood what No Exit actually is.

It's a prison.

A prison where rules apply.

If you don't follow them, there are sanctions.

I glance at Gwen, who's standing beside me.

"Eyes front, Twenty-Five A!" one of the guards yells. I'm already used to my number, because I know right away that the guard means me.

At that moment, someone comes down the staircase.

"Welcome!" Tina's supersweet voice echoes around the deck. She stops on the third step again, looking down on us. "Welcome to No Exit. Everyone is here, I see? Sorry about the awkward start. I hope we can soon put that behind us."

As she says the last sentence, Tina's gaze briefly rests on Jonah. He's standing upright, but I know it must be painful. Harrold hit him so hard.

"I understand that there are a lot of questions, and that's what I'm here for. I will be your contact person during your stay."

Stay.

Tina is still making it sound as if this is a luxury cruise.

"So, are there any questions?"

Jonah raises his hand. Tina tries to ignore him, but he's the only one, so she has to let him speak.

"Yes, Eight B?"

"What are you guys going to do if someone pees in the pool? That wasn't mentioned in the folder."

It's like the whole group holds its breath. Why is Jonah doing this? Has he forgotten the beating he just got?

"Then there will be sanctions," Tina says calmly.

"And what do those sanctions involve?" Jonah asks.

"I believe you've already become acquainted with them, haven't you?"

"Sure." Jonah glances at Harrold. "And if that doesn't work?"

"Then they get more serious." Tina smiles. "Any other questions?"

Luckily, Jonah is silent. I don't want to think about that guard beating up on him again.

"Fine, if there are no more questions"—Tina claps her hands—"then it's time for lunch."

Lunch . . .

How am I supposed to eat in a place like this?

But my rumbling stomach convinces me, and I fill my tray with fruit salad, fresh tomatoes, bread rolls, and a bowl of yogurt.

"Do you want a white roll or a brown one?" I ask Gwen.

"Give me a brown one."

When I've handed it to her, she brings it to her face and gives it a sniff.

"What are you doing?"

"Checking if you're honest," Gwen replies with a smile. "Seems I can trust you."

"Keep walking, ladies." Jumper is standing just behind us. "You're holding up the line."

He pokes Gwen in the back and I see her stiffen.

"Hey, take it easy," I say. "We're moving."

I add Gwen's food to my tray and she holds my arm. I guide her between the tables and make a beeline for Jonah, who's sitting by the window.

"Vesper." He nods. "Or should I say . . ."

"Twenty-Five A." I drop down into the chair across from him. "You okay?"

"Yep." Jonah's eyes light up. "I am now."

"I'm Twenty-Five B." Gwen holds out her hand and knocks into Jonah's glass. The water splashes all over his cheese sandwich.

"Oh, sorry!" Gwen blushes. "Did I just ruin your lunch?"

"No, it's all good." Jonah holds up his dripping sandwich and glances at me. "No damage done."

My gaze flashes to Tina, who's standing quite a distance away from us. There's no guard nearby.

If I want to talk to Jonah, I have to do it now.

"Jonah." I lean forward. "How did you know this wasn't a vacation?"

"What do you mean?" Jonah says, giving me an innocent look.

"You asked me who wanted to get rid of me. Remember? The whole 'hellhole' conversation?"

Jonah nods. "And I was mistaken. I mean, the food is delicious, and the rooms are delightful. My roommate is perhaps a little . . ."

"What do you know about No Exit?" I insist.

"Enough." Jonah takes a bite of his sandwich. "You guys?"

"I've heard some stories." Gwen starts her salad. "But I don't know how true they are."

"What kind of stories?" I ask.

"Well, I heard that not everyone . . ." She stops, and her face clouds over.

"What?"

"Oh, that." Jonah nods. "I've heard that rumor!"

"What rumor?" I have to suppress the urge to scream. "Just tell me."

Gwen puts down her fork. "Rumor has it that not everyone makes it back alive."

2. OPEN SEA

DIARY OF ▬▬▬▬▬▬▬

There are days when I want to kill him. And days when I want to kill myself.
   I would love to escape ▬▬▬▬▬▬
   But I'm stuck ▬▬

Ultimately, I don't think I could ever do that.
   Suicide, I mean.

VESPER

Rumor has it that not everyone makes it back alive.

"You okay?" Jonah asks when I don't react.

"That's not possible," I say.

"Of course it is." Jonah looks around. "Anything is possible here."

"But surely not without any consequences? I mean, the government . . . and my dad. He'd never have signed me up for this if he thought that . . ."

"They'll obviously tell them a different story." Jonah's smile is still there. "If someone dies, it'll be a 'tragic accident.'"

I feel my stomach flip.

"Anyway, there's too much evidence that the program works. Anyone who makes it through No Exit will think twice before they bully someone again."

"But what about the ship? Who's paying for all this?"

"Ted." Jonah leans forward a little. "The captain, the guy on TV. He's apparently a billionaire."

"It's pretty smart," says Gwen. "A ship like this. There's nowhere to go. We're miles from anywhere."

"So that others will be safe." Jonah perfectly imitates the voice in the video. It gives me chills.

I try to process the information, but I can't take it in. People have died, but this program is allowed to continue? Ted and his team keep teenage prisoners on this ship and . . .

And what, exactly? We still don't know what the "phases" are all about. Karma and confrontation?

What's going to happen?

"Everyone wants to get rid of us," Jonah continues. "School, parents, the government . . . They'll do whatever it takes to change us. But first they have to break us."

"What do you mean?"

"That's the order they do it in." Jonah puts up three fingers. "Break you, reshape you, and hand you back. With some people, that takes a lot of work."

He glances at a nearby table, where Jumper is sitting with a large group. "Some people are rotten through and through."

"And if that doesn't work, they just *kill* you?" I can't imagine it. How could that be possible?

"Exactly. If we don't make enough of an improvement,

they throw us overboard. 'Oops, it was an accident! She was standing too close to the edge and there was a big wave, Your Honor.'"

"Don't be so weird."

"I believe it," Gwen says quietly. "No one's going to miss a bully."

"You said you were innocent, didn't you?"

"Of course she's innocent," says Jonah.

"Why do you say that?"

"Because she . . ." Jonah's gaze rests on Gwen's eyes for a moment. "Because she's way too nice."

"I *am* innocent," says Gwen. "But on board this ship, I'm as much of a bully as the rest of you. There's no way they're going to let me off."

She strokes the number on her uniform.

"What's going to happen?" I ask Jonah. "What are they going to do to us?"

"I don't know." Jonah downs the water that was left in his glass. "It's different every year."

"And how do you know that?"

"From witness accounts," Jonah says vaguely.

"Did you read them online or something?"

"Nope." Jonah shakes his head. "If a former participant leaks the smallest detail about No Exit to the media, they know where to find you."

"So how do you know it's different every year?"

"From my brothers." Jonah looks at me. "They both survived No Exit."

"Both of his brothers . . ." Gwen is walking down the corridor beside me.

"Yes," I say. "Bizarre, huh?"

I wanted to go on talking to Jonah, but just as I was about to ask him how on earth he'd followed the same path as his brothers, Tina sent us back to our cabins.

I see Jonah go into cabin 8.

Gwen and I walk on to the end of the corridor. With every step I take, I feel more anxious and claustrophobic.

When we're back in the cabin, it might be hours before we're allowed out again.

And the windows don't open.

How could I ever have seen this ship as something beautiful?

I stop at the door, after Gwen has gone in.

I can't do it. I don't want to be locked in again.

"Twenty-Five A!" Harrold the guard comes striding toward me. "Inside. Now!"

Why did Dad send me here?

Doesn't he know about the scary rumors?

Or is he so messed up after Mom's death that he doesn't care if I die too?

No, that's not possible. I'm all that Dad has left.

"Twenty-Five A." The guard has almost reached me.

"Vesper!" Gwen reaches out and finds my arm. Just before Harrold gets to me, she pulls me inside and the door slides shut behind me.

"Why did you just stand there?" Gwen yells at me. "You know what they'll do, don't you?"

I'm about to tell her that it doesn't matter anymore, that people might actually die here, when I look around the cabin.

"No . . ."

Gwen turns around. "What's wrong?"

I dive toward my bed, where my backpack is. It's badly damaged—the fabric has been slashed in several places.

My clothes, swimming gear, towel have all been cut to pieces. The pages of my book have been shredded and scattered across the floor.

"Mom . . ." I look around in panic. Where is she?

"Hello there, Bullies." The screen flashes on. Ted smiles into the cabin. "Welcome to the karmic phase."

My eyes dart to the folder. Karmic phase . . .

"Ah, karma. You've probably heard the word before. It means that whatever you do will come back to you one day.

And in this case, to each and every one of you. In the coming days, your deeds will literally return to all of you. Do you know who you have to thank for what's just happened? Nine A! So, make sure to say thanks when you see her!"

And then the screen goes black again.

"No . . ." I drop to my knees and look under the bed. It has to be here somewhere, but where?

"What's going on?" Gwen says, groping around. "What has Nine A done?"

"My things," I say. "They're all ruined."

"Ruined?" Gwen's face turns pale. "Everything?"

"All my personal stuff!" I jump to my feet and open the closet. Where have they put it?

Gwen goes to her own room and comes back with red cheeks. "My things . . ."

"I know!"

"What are you doing now?"

"I'm looking for something!" I run to the bathroom, but there's no sign of it in there either. There are only two bars of soap lying neatly on two snow-white towels.

Why have they done this? How could they?

"What are you looking for?" Gwen manages to find my arm and holds on to me tightly. "Vesper, what's missing?"

"My mom." I feel sick. "I'm looking for the urn with my mom's ashes inside."

* * *

"We'll find it." Gwen keeps repeating the same thing, but I can barely hear her.

I'm sitting on the bed with my legs pulled up and my arms wrapped around them.

Mom's gone. Really gone.

It's like she just died for the second time.

"As soon as we can, we'll ask Tina if she knows where..."

"Of course. She must have taken it." I look up. "Because she wants to break me. Jonah said that's what they'd do!"

"But they can't do that, can they?" Gwen says, shaking her head. "They can't just confiscate an urn."

"People actually die here," I remind her.

"That's just a rumor," Gwen says quickly.

"You just said you believed it! You said no one would miss a bully."

Gwen turns red and falls silent.

I try to picture Dad's face when I tell him what's happened. I should have left Mom on the bookcase, safe in the living room.

I look at Gwen, who has a torn photograph in her hand. Suddenly I realize that her things have been destroyed as well.

"Who is it a photograph of?" I ask.

"Rixt," says Gwen. "Rixt and me."

"Is that your sister?"

Gwen nods. "Sort of. She was actually my best friend, but she felt just like a sister."

I notice that she uses the past tense.

"Is she dead?"

Gwen nods. She looks down. I know she's not seeing it, but it's as if she's staring at the photograph.

"So . . . why do you have a photo with you if you can't see it?"

Gwen smiles. "I can feel her."

"Is it a braille photo?"

Gwen bursts out laughing. "A *what*?"

"Braille is an alphabet you can feel, isn't it? I thought there might be braille photos that you can feel with your fingertips too."

"No." Gwen shakes her head and laughs. "But there really should be such a thing."

"Can I see Rixt?"

I put the halves of the photo together and look at it. The tear runs precisely through Gwen and Rixt, as if someone really wanted to give Gwen some extra pain.

Did Tina do this herself? No, she can't have, because she was at lunch the whole time. She must have told a guard to do the dirty work.

I look at the girl on the left. Rixt has long dark hair hanging in waves over her shoulders. She has perfect skin with a small birthmark on one cheek. Her big smile shows a line of perfectly white teeth, and her eyes . . . There's something about her eyes.

They're not as panicky as Gwen's, but they're not really happy either.

Far from it, in fact.

"Was she unhappy?" I hear myself ask.

Gwen looks up in surprise. "Why do you say that?"

"She looks sad." I hand the photo back to her. "How did she die?"

Gwen sighs. There's a brief silence, which I know only too well. Whenever people start talking about Mom, I always use that moment of silence to prepare myself. Armor on. Buckle up.

But when I reply, it still feels as if I'm falling to pieces.

"You don't have . . . ," I begin, but then Gwen takes a deep breath.

"She was murdered."

I feel my jaw dropping. "Oh . . ."

Murder.

That kind of thing only happens in the movies, doesn't it?

"It's okay," says Gwen, stuffing the two halves of the photo into her pocket. I know she's trying to be brave—that's something that feels familiar too.

But her best friend was murdered. Of course it's not okay.

"How did your mom die?" asks Gwen. Something else that feels familiar. Always change the subject as quickly as you can.

This time I'm the one who falls silent. Armor on. Buckle up.

"Cancer," I say, feeling the blow again. It's as if that word sucks all the energy out of the room. "Not as bad as yours."

Gwen looks up. "Dead is dead, isn't it?"

Yes, but *murder*? Some days it feels like Mom was murdered too, but of course that's not the case.

She wanted to euthanize herself.

But Death had already been around for days. Almost literally. At first he stood at the front door. Mom let him in.

He lingered in the hallway for a while. Mom started getting sentimental. She kept telling me what a big girl I was, even though I felt smaller than ever.

Then Death was in the living room. Mom asked all kinds of visitors to come over—family, friends—and the house became busier and busier.

And eventually Death sat down on the edge of her bed, right beside me. Mom spent more and more time asleep.

Sometimes I watched her for hours, trying to imagine

what it would be like when she didn't wake up again. How it would feel.

"Why did you have the urn with you?" Gwen says, pulling me out of my thoughts.

"I wanted to scatter her ashes. My dad didn't. He said she belonged with us. But I took her anyway, because Mom loved the sea. She doesn't belong on a bookcase, does she? But now . . ." I wince. "Now she's gone. I stole her from Dad, and No Exit has stolen her from me. Now, that's what I call karma."

The karmic phase has begun. They've stolen and destroyed our personal belongings.

Apparently, 9A did that to someone.

I remember the girl. She was the one who winced when Jonah got hit. She looked more scared than anything else, not like someone who would destroy someone's stuff.

"All Bullies, step away from the door!"

Gwen and I both jump up at once. When the door slides open, we're looking into the face of a guard.

"Twenty-Five A and Twenty-Five B, come with me!"

"Why?" I ask, but there's no answer. In the corridor, I see all the others standing in front of their doors. Luckily, Jonah's done as he was told this time. He looks at us and smiles.

"Bullies, follow me." The guard goes ahead of us down

the long corridor. This time we're heading not to the foredeck but in the opposite direction.

"What are we going to do?" I ask, but the man doesn't seem to hear me.

"They're taking us to the back of the ship," I say to Gwen, who's holding my arm. Every time we turn a corner and she starts to lose her footing, her nails dig into my skin through my uniform.

"Silence, Twenty-Five A," growls the guard in front of us.

As we step outside, the sun shines full in my face. Weirdly, for a moment, I feel free, as if we're just on vacation. The fresh breeze, the steel-blue sea, the sun loungers . . .

At the same time, I hate that thought, because I know this is most definitely not a vacation.

And then I see Tina standing by the railing. Without thinking, I run over to her.

"Tina! Where's the urn that was in my cabin?"

Tina doesn't even look at me. She just looks the other way, as if I don't exist. As if I'm nothing more than a number.

"It was an *urn*!" I grab her arm. "You can't do that!"

Then I feel a hand on my collar, and someone pulls me away from Tina. I fall back onto the deck, banging my head on one of the loungers.

The guard glares down at me.

"Cool it, Twenty-Five A," he growls.

"Leave her," I hear Tina say. "Do you need me to help you up, Twenty-Five A?"

My head is pounding, but I scramble to my feet. No way am I going to let Tina help me.

"So, something's gone missing from your room?" Tina asks in her sickly sweet voice. "How annoying."

Annoying? That's when you leave the house without a coat and you get caught in a rain shower. Or when you get home from shopping and realize you've forgotten the most important ingredient for dinner.

Losing an urn with your mom's ashes in it? That's way more than annoying.

"But that's no reason for you to disturb everyone's peace," Tina says before turning to the others. "Okay, Bullies," she says. "Welcome to the rear deck of the ship. I hope you're enjoying the beautiful view."

I look at Jonah, whose eyes are fixed on 9A. And I see now that he's not the only one. Half of the group is staring furiously at her.

Do you know who you have to thank for what's just happened? 9A! So, make sure to say thanks when you see her!

Suddenly I realize the effect of Ted's comment. It's made everyone hate 9A.

The only one who seems to be protecting her is her

roommate, 9B, a big guy with blond curls and muscular arms.

He's standing in front of her, as if he's planning to knock down anyone who's thinking of attacking her.

"You okay?" asks Gwen. "Did you hit something when you fell?"

I rub the back of my head. Compared to the beating that Jonah took, this is nothing. The pain is already fading.

"I'm fine," I say. "But the whole group hates Nine A now."

"Because it was her karma?" Gwen frowns. "That's so dumb. She wasn't the one who ruined our stuff, was she? That was No Exit!"

"Exactly." I crack my knuckles.

"Hey, you are not going to start fighting." Gwen suddenly sounds stern. "Simmer down."

"Yeah, yeah."

"I mean it," says Gwen. "I need you."

"To read information sheets to you?"

"To *survive* this place," says Gwen. "No one survives prison on their own."

I remember a documentary I watched the other day. In every prison, people make friends. Even in the most awful circumstances, prisoners become closer to one another.

In fact, it's the awful circumstances that bring them together.

"I'm not going to do anything stupid," I promise.

"Everyone, come and stand on the railing. We're going to have a *Titanic* moment."

When no one moves, a guard pushes 9A forward. The girl looks anxiously at her cellmate, but then she walks to the railing. As she steps onto the bottom bar, she looks at Tina, who nods approvingly.

Tina looks at the group. "Now the rest of you."

Slowly, everyone follows her example. Within a few seconds, we're all standing on the railing, like Jack in *Titanic*. I remember the scene where he spreads his arms and shouts that he's the king of the world. I feel like anything but.

Gwen is clutching the railing, as if she might fall at any moment. Maybe that's how it feels for her.

I close my eyes for a moment. And immediately my other senses sharpen: I feel the wind in my hair, I smell the salty sea air, and feel the water splashing onto my face.

Tiny little droplets, which I didn't feel before.

Everything is so much more intense.

And scarier.

I sway, almost losing my balance.

I'm about to open my eyes again when I suddenly feel two hands on my ankles. Something snaps into place, and then I'm lifted up.

Before I can even shout for help, I get thrown over the railing.

DIARY OF ▬▬▬▬▬▬

He just sent me a message.
　I have no idea how he got my number.
　　My friends offered me 100 bucks if I kiss you.
　　I'm so scared that he knows, ▬▬

—

I feel so powerless.
　I just wish I could go to ▬▬▬▬▬▬▬▬▬▬▬▬▬▬▬▬▬
▬▬▬▬▬▬▬▬▬▬
▬▬▬▬▬▬▬

VESPER

It takes me a second to realize what's going on.

And then I scream. I scream so loud that it feels like my eardrums are about to burst.

The water is coming toward me, just a huge, blue surface, and then . . .

I go under. My scream is drowned by the seawater, and I taste salt.

I'm going to die.

This is it.

They're going to kill me.

The rope on my ankles pulls tight, but they're not pulling up.

I struggle, but there's no point. I'm being dragged along beneath the water. The ship is sailing so fast that I don't stand a chance.

Weirdly, I know that right away.

Dad, I'm sorry.

I never should have taken Mom.

I hope I get to tell you that one day.

You were a pretty good dad. I know that's not what I always said, but I was mad at you. Because you were still there, and Mom was gone.

I was a mommy's girl. You know that.

The water is everywhere, swallowing me, choking me. How did I ever think this blue water was beautiful?

Sorry, Dad.

Sorry.

Sorry.

Sor . . .

And then they pull me up. Gasping for breath, I'm back above water and I can see the blue sea below.

I gave up so quickly, but my fighting spirit returns just as fast.

I can survive this.

I'm not going to die!

"Help!" I scream again. "Pull me up!" But then I go plummeting back down.

Again, I take in a mouthful of seawater, choking and spluttering. I want to cough, but I can't.

Pull me up.

Please, pull me up.

And then they haul me up again.

As soon as I'm above the water, I start coughing. It feels like I'm puking up my lungs.

"Tina," I manage to say.

I know there's no point. No one's going to hear me above the roar of the waves as they pound against the side of the ship.

The noise takes my breath away.

The ocean is going to swallow me up.

If they lower me one more time, I'm not going to survive.

"Please . . ."

And then I start going down again.

No.

No, not again.

But even now, I'm still alive.

Even the next three times, I'm still alive.

My heart goes on beating. It doesn't care about what's going on inside my head.

When I get pulled back up yet again, I start preparing for the next dose of seawater. But this time they pull me up higher.

I see the water farther and farther below. I'm like the hanging plant in our living room.

I feel two strong hands on my upper arms, and then I get tossed onto the deck.

The sun stings my face. My heart is thudding painfully, but I suck in oxygen as if I'm addicted to it.

"Ah, you're back," Tina's voice, even sweeter than her perfume, whispers into my ear. "You need to stop making such a scene," she says. "Promise?"

Is that why she threw me overboard? Because I wanted my mom's urn back?

I want to scream again. I want to turn that shot of oxygen into curse words. But then I hear Gwen's voice inside my head.

Simmer down. I need you.

Someone helps me to my feet. I lean on the railing, gasping.

"Vesper." It's Gwen. "Y-you okay?"

"Tina tried to kill me." I look at Gwen, who is as white as a sheet. Did she realize what happened?

"No," says Gwen.

"Don't you know what she did? She just basically keelhauled me!"

"It was an exercise."

"In what?" I spit seawater onto the deck. "Obedience?"

"You weren't the only one." Gwen nudges me. "Look around." When I look up, I see Jumper standing nearby. Jonah's cellmate is soaked through. He's doubled over, vomiting seawater.

And then I see some more. 13B and 19A, both of them dripping wet.

Tina's voice rises above the sea breeze. "That was your second encounter with the karmic phase."

What is she saying now?

I think about the ruined things in our room.

9A once destroyed someone's belongings, so we had to suffer the same fate.

Karmic phase . . .

Does that mean someone in this group held someone underwater?

Who would do such a horrible thing?

I look around the group.

"Ma'am!" Harrold's loud voice startles me. He's crouching on the ground some distance away. "We have an exit!"

An exit? What's that?

But then I see the girl. She's slumped against the railing, her wet hair hanging over her face like tentacles.

4B, it says on her uniform.

"Resuscitate." Tina's voice is suddenly forceful, businesslike.

The guard lays the girl flat on her back and starts slamming her chest.

I feel like I'm back underwater.

All the air gets knocked out of my lungs.

"Come on," I hear Harrold. "Come on, you bitch." He keeps pressing.

Push, push, push, stop.

He breathes into her mouth and starts again.

Push, push, push, stop.

Nothing happens.

Gwen has grabbed my arm again and is digging her nails into my flesh.

For the first time, I wish I were blind.

I don't want to see this.

But I can't look away.

After what feels like an eternity, Harrold looks up. His face is bright red and dripping with sweat. He wipes his sleeve over his eyes.

"She's dead."

For a moment, it's so silent on deck that all I can hear is my own breathing.

I'm still breathing.

And she isn't.

"You did your best" is all Tina says. She snaps her fingers. "All Bullies to the foredeck. There's nothing to see here."

"She's dead."

They're the only words I can hear on the foredeck. Everyone is huddled in small groups.

"She's dead. Actually dead . . ."

Then more words are added.

"I don't even know what her name was."

"What does her name matter? She's been murdered!"

"No Exit is killing us!"

I don't say anything myself.

I have a towel around my shoulders that a guard gave me. Gwen and I are sitting on the ground, leaning against one of the walls.

Gwen has let go of my arm and found my hand.

I've known this girl for only a few hours and she's clutching my hand as if I'm her life buoy.

But she's mine as well.

If she lets go of me now, then I'm really going to drown.

"They left Four B underwater way too long!"

"Yeah, I noticed that too. The others got pulled up a few times. They only brought her up once!"

I remember the times I came up above water. Gasping for breath, getting ready for the next round.

Did they give this girl only one chance?

"There weren't enough guards," someone says. "You saw that, didn't you? Five people got thrown overboard, but there were only four guys to keep bringing them back up."

"So why didn't you do something?"

"Like what? That Tina woman said we'd be next if we . . ."

I miss half of what they're saying.

"If I ever find out which one of us did this . . ."

"What do you mean?"

"Karmic phase. That means one of us . . . So that's who we have to thank for this!"

Someone starts crying—and then something snaps inside my head. I turn to look at the girl who's sobbing.

"Stop it!" I spit out the words. "Stop crying!"

The girl glares at me through her tears. "Mind your own business?"

"Stop crying," I say again. "It's not going to bring anyone back."

"So?" Her face is so wet that it looks like she was just pulled out of the water too. I see *4A* on her uniform. 4B was her cellmate. "I'll cry if I want to."

Her voice is trembling.

My vision blurs. My hands are shaking.

Three, two, one . . .

But then Gwen steps in.

"What Vesper means is that we need to stop blaming each other. Half an hour ago we were all ready to attack 9A because of what happened to our stuff, and now we're already after the next victim. It's No Exit doing this to us. No one else."

"And who are you?" I hear someone ask. When I look

up, I see Jumper sitting there. He's still soaked from head to toe, and he's wrapped up in a white towel too.

"I'm Gwen."

"Well, Gwen, you've got it wrong. Thanks to one of us, I nearly died, and I want to know who's to blame."

Jumper gives a loud sniff.

"I know you're not seeing it clearly, but"—he pauses—"but why don't you just shut up?"

"Sorry?" The black haze before my eyes slowly gives way to red. "*What* did you say?"

"That the blind girl needs to shut her mouth."

"No, you do!" I say, but Jumper isn't impressed.

"So, who are you?"

"Vesper," I say. "And you're Jumper. Right?"

He runs a hand through his wet hair. His blue eyes remind me of the water that almost killed me just now.

"Yeah." Jumper laughs. "And if you knew *why* people call me that . . ."

Before I can say anything, he stands up. "Come on, guys. Those two don't get it. And now that we finally have a bit of free time, we can go wherever we like."

Gwen and I sit on the deck for a while, just the two of us, and then something suddenly occurs to me.

"Hey, where's Jonah?"

I haven't seen him since 4B died. Has he gone to his cabin? Is he sitting there on his own?

No one should be alone right now.

"I'm going to go look for him."

"I'm staying here," says Gwen. "I'll see you later."

I check his cabin first, then the pool, but he's not there either. Even the restaurant is deserted.

I refuse to go back to the rear deck. 4B might still be there.

I walk all the way to the top deck of the ship. The wind is blowing even harder up there, but there's no sign of Jonah.

Where can he be?

When I want to be alone, I usually lock myself away in the bathroom, but I don't find him there.

And then I think about Dad.

When he fled the house after Mom died, there was always one place I could find him.

I take a deep breath and walk across the red carpet to the casino. As soon as I see the lights and hear the sounds, my stomach does a flip.

But I go on walking.

And then I see him.

Jonah is standing at one of the slot machines, one hand on the lever, the other on the machine.

"Come on," I hear him shout. "Come on!"

I see Harrold in front of me, trying to resuscitate 4B. The guard said exactly the same thing, with the addition of "you bitch." They might have been the last words the girl ever heard.

"Jonah."

When he hears his name, Jonah looks up. His eyes are wild.

Dad sometimes looked like that when I went to fetch him. Like he couldn't believe there was someone at home who missed him.

"What are you doing?"

"I'm winning." Jonah points at the machine.

"No one ever wins with those things. That's how they're set up. You know that, right?"

Jonah shakes his head. "I win."

He turns back and pulls the lever. I slowly move closer.

"How much money have you put in there?" I ask.

"Nearly everything I've got." Jonah doesn't look at me, keeps his eyes fixed on the display.

I look at the numbers on the screen. He doesn't have many tries left.

Three sevens appear. The fourth picture is a lemon.

"See. Looks like life is giving you lemons," I say dryly.

"Just need one more." Jonah's eyes are blazing.

"There's no point," I say. "Stop now or you're going to lose everything."

But Jonah pulls the lever again. The lemon disappears and I see other symbols flashing by. Then it stops.

Four sevens.

"Yes!" Jonah throws his arms in the air.

The machine makes a happy noise and there's a jingling sound. Jonah's red numbers rattle up to a high amount.

"Jackpot!" He looks at me with a grin. "Told you so!" He's right—this time.

"Now you need to stop," I say.

"Stop? Why? Just when it's finally going well?" Jonah tugs the lever and the game begins again.

"Why did you come here?" I ask.

"To win some money."

"That girl," I begin. "I just keep seeing her in front of me."

"Is that why you came looking for me? To talk about that?" Jonah's expression hardens. "Go talk to Gwen."

"She didn't see it," I say. "You did."

"Barely." Jonah pulls the lever again. "That fat guard was in the way."

Three sevens appear again, but this time the last symbol is a bunch of grapes, and it doesn't budge. The red numbers go back down.

"Why don't you give it a go?" Jonah steps aside.

I stare at the lever and frantically shake my head. "No way."

"Why not? It's fun." Jonah pulls me up to the slot machine

and places my hand on the lever. When he brings it down, I see the new symbols appearing.

"I can't do this," I say, letting go of the lever.

Jonah snorts. "Anyone can do this. It's brainless."

"So why do you do it, then?"

"Because I want to be brainless for a while." Jonah takes the lever again. "Don't you?"

"Maybe."

I think about 4B. Have her parents been informed yet? And what will No Exit tell them? That it was an accident, just like Jonah said they would?

"Do you think she was dead when she hit the water?"

"Vesper!" Jonah slams his fist on the machine. "Go talk to Gwen. Please!"

"No." I cross my arms. "I want to talk to you."

"Why?"

"You do not want to know what's happening up on deck right now. Everyone's looking for the person they think is to blame for this. Don't you understand? No Exit is turning us against each other. Jumper's really mad and . . ."

Jonah pulls the lever again. The last symbol disappears—and then it's finally over.

"Bust," he says, letting go of the lever. "You were right."

"What about?"

Jonah smiles. "I've lost everything."

* * *

"Jonah was being weird." I'm lying on my bed. Gwen is sitting on the floor, leaning against the wall. We were brought back to our cabins a half hour ago and the door is locked again.

My stomach's rumbling. I should have eaten something in those few hours of free time.

"Weird how?"

"Well, less Labradorish."

"What?"

"Like a Labrador. You know, all bouncy and happy."

I think of Ollie. It feels like I haven't seen him in years.

"Someone died," says Gwen. "No one's Labradorish anymore."

Maybe she's right. So why does it feel like I've missed something important about Jonah?

"Attention, Bullies." Ted's face appears on the screen again. He looks paler than before.

"Bullies, we are taking a moment to reflect on the passing of Four B. What happened is terrible, but of course you've all created your own victims. So it's hardly surprising that a victim has fallen on your side now, too."

Did he really just say that? As if 4B deserved it!

Karma.

That man is seriously disturbed. I want to reach into the screen and attack him.

"And to the Bullies who survived: you have one of your own to thank for that little dip in the ocean."

I don't want to hear it.

I don't care whose karma this was.

Even though I nearly drowned, the one who threw me overboard is the only one who's to blame.

It's No Exit that did this. No one else.

"The Bully in question once held a classmate underwater for minutes," Ted calmly continues. "He gave him a few pauses to gasp for breath, but not long."

I think about the water, swallowing me like a predator.

And I see 4B before me, limp and dead.

Come on, you bitch.

"I'm sure you'd like to know who it was. I get it."

I imagine Jumper sitting upright in his cabin now, waiting for the number.

Whoever it is, they're not safe. Jumper's going to attack them, maybe even kill them. "The Bully you have to thank for this is . . . Eight B."

Jonah.

It's like the pieces of the puzzle are falling into place.

As if the last number seven finally appeared on my screen.

Because I want to be brainless for a while.

Suddenly I realize the important signal I was missing.

"No . . . ," I whisper, and I see that Gwen has realized too. "Jonah's in the same cabin as Jumper!"

DIARY OF

Right in the middle of the schoolyard, he put his hand on my chest.

His gross, disgusting hand gave it a squeeze.

And as he did it, he looked at me.

DON'T CRY.

VESPER

It was Jonah.

Because of Jonah, I was held underwater for minutes.

Because of Jonah's karma, 4B is now dead.

I remember his fixed expression as he went on pulling the lever.

Stop now or you're going to lose everything, I'd said, but he just kept on going.

Why should he care?

He'd already lost everything.

As soon as the five of us were thrown overboard, he must have realized it was *his* karma.

And when they couldn't resuscitate 4B. I gag.

"Vesper." Gwen's voice brings me back to the moment. "Vesper, stay calm."

"Calm?" I splutter. "Jonah is in the same cabin as Jumper."

"I know." Gwen's expression is serious.

"That guy is going to kill him." I remember the anger in Jumper's voice when we were up on deck. "We need to help Jonah."

"How do you think you're going to do that? We're trapped in here!"

"Tina!" I know there's no point, but I have to try something. I start banging on the door and yelling at the top of my voice.

Why isn't Gwen helping? The two of us would make way more noise. Someone must be able to hear us!

I turn around and see that Gwen is lying on the floor. Her body is shaking uncontrollably.

What's going on?

"Gwen!" I hurry over to her. Her limbs seem to have a life of their own—they're flailing in all directions.

"Gwen!" I try to hold her, but her foot hits my arm.

Is she dying?

No, she can't be, she can't!

I need you.

"Gwen!" My voice catches in my throat. "Can you hear me? Gwen!"

"Bullies, step away from the door." I barely hear the voice from outside. But suddenly Gwen looks right at me for a moment.

"Key card. Jonah" is all she whispers. And then she starts shaking again.

"Twenty-Five A, step aside." The guard grabs Gwen and rolls her onto her side. He holds her tightly so she can't bump into anything.

I look at the scene in front of me. The guard has a belt with a . . . key card!

Suddenly I realize what Gwen meant. She just faked an attack so that . . .

I grab the card from his belt and start running.

I wait for the alarm, for the firm hand to land on my shoulder and throw me back into my cabin, but that doesn't happen.

When I get to cabin 8, I slip the key card into the reader. The light turns green, and the door slides open.

"Jonah." But I see at once that the room is empty.

There's no sign of Jonah or Jumper.

How is that possible? Has No Exit moved them somewhere else? Because they knew all hell would break loose as soon as Jumper found out that his roommate was supposedly to blame for his near-death experience?

But then I hear muffled sounds coming from the bathroom.

I pull the door open and feel my body freeze.

Jumper is standing by the toilet, holding Jonah by the

back of his neck. He's pushing him so far into the bowl that I know his face must be touching the water.

"Jonah!"

Jumper looks up. When he sees me, his expression moves swiftly from surprise to fury.

"What are you doing here?"

"Let go of him!" I run at him, but Jumper gives me a hard shove. Then he pulls Jonah up for a moment. Jonah spits out water and coughs.

"That's how it feels, pal. And here we go again!" Jumper pushes Jonah's head back into the toilet. I can hear him gagging and coughing. Water splashes up over the toilet seat.

"Now, that's what I call a karmic phase." Jumper laughs as he pulls Jonah up. "Right, Jonah?"

"Stop it!" I yell, but Jumper's not listening.

"I nearly died. And it's all your fault! You fucking rat." Jumper pushes him underwater again.

I look around and see the metal garbage bin in the corner. Without thinking, I snatch it off the floor.

With all my strength, I bring the bin down on Jumper's head.

"Twenty-Five A and Eight A." Tina is looking at Jumper and me from behind a large desk. Her fingers are tapping on the glass surface. "This incident will naturally have consequences."

I glance to the side. Jumper is holding a packet of frozen peas to his forehead, right where I hit him with the garbage bin. The whack I gave him was enough to bring him down. Jonah came up from the toilet bowl, coughing and spluttering.

Then Harrold stormed into the cabin and took Jumper and me with him.

"We have a zero-tolerance policy for violence on this ship."

I look up. Is Tina serious?

Simmer down, Gwen's voice says inside my head. *I need you.*

"We are a reeducation program. But you are not supposed to carry out that education yourself." She looks at me, then Jumper, and back at me.

"We have a zero-tolerance policy for violence."

"I don't know if Four B would agree with that."

The comment is out before Gwen's voice in my head can warn me.

The silence in the room is unbearable, but I go on staring right at Tina. *Someone* had to say it. It's bad enough that 4B was murdered. And the way No Exit hides behind the idea of "reeducation" is too disgusting for words.

Tina stares back at me. My eyes start to burn, but I refuse to blink. No way I'm going to be the first to give up.

And then Tina finally looks away.

Won that one, I think.

"Ted?" Tina presses a button on her desk.

"Yes?" says a man's voice, which I know only too well from the screen.

"I have a Wrecker here."

For a moment, I think she got my name wrong, but then I realize what she actually said.

"Who is it?" Ted asks.

"Twenty-Five A." Tina glances up at me. "The girl with the urn."

My heart does a little skip.

"Ah," he says. "Send her to me."

Then he breaks the connection.

"You heard him." Tina's smile is back. Suddenly I realize that No Exit is one big slot machine. In this place, you can only lose. "Ted wants to speak to you."

The room I'm sent to is empty.

When I look over my shoulder, I see that the guard has already closed the door. And when I try the handle, it doesn't budge.

I'm locked in.

Of course.

"Twenty-Five A," Ted's voice booms through the room.

I turn around, but there's no one there—just a 2D Ted on a large screen on the wall.

"Sit down."

I look back at the door, but there's no point. I have to obey. Reluctantly, I drop onto the chair.

"So, you're a Wrecker, are you?" Ted asks. His piercing eyes won't let me go. I don't understand how someone can be so good-looking and so scary at the same time.

"I don't know what you mean," I say.

"A Wrecker is someone who endangers our project." Ted goes on staring at me. "Are you a danger, Twenty-Five A?"

"No."

"Then why did Tina say you were?"

"Because I escaped from my cabin."

"And how did you manage to do that?"

I remember Gwen's fake attack. No way I'm going to snitch on her.

"My roommate had an epileptic fit, and a guard came. He left the door open."

"And what did you do then?"

"I went to cabin eight. Because of Jonah. Jumper was attacking him because—"

"Prisoner names, please."

"Eight A was attacking Eight B," I say reluctantly.

Ted nods slowly.

"Because of your *karmic phase*." I say the last two words with extra emphasis.

Ted steeples his fingers. "Do you believe that No Exit is the correct approach to rehabilitation?"

I snort. Is he serious?

"Of course not! You murder people."

Ted doesn't even blink. It's as if he's weighing my words.

"There was a casualty, that's true. Because of Eight B's actions, she—"

"Because of *you*!"

"No, because of all of *you*." Ted isn't shouting, but somehow the air is still vibrating. "Because of people like *you*, millions of victims are terrified every year. You exclude them, insult them, ridicule them, destroy their belongings, hold them underwater as a so-called joke, and, let me see . . ." Ted leans across the camera and a dark-blue folder appears on-screen. I glimpse my name on the front as he opens it. "In front of half the school, you make people—"

"I know what I did," I say quickly.

Ted looks up. "Good." Luckily, he closes the folder. "Then you know what I mean. People like you destroy others. And bullying is only possible because there are no serious penalties for it. That needs to change. You understand that, don't you? At No Exit, we make sure the bullying stops. Research has shown that people learn from their mistakes most quickly when the same thing happens to them. Call it an eye for an eye. Karma."

"That makes no sense."

"Is that so?" Ted smiles. "Didn't you get really mad when this disappeared?"

My blood freezes when he holds up the urn.

Mom.

"You can't . . ." Dozens of swear words are stuck inside my head. "You can't do that kind of thing."

"Maybe not. But if we'd done it to someone else, you wouldn't have cared. Right?"

He stole my urn. Or got someone else to steal it.

And she's with him.

My mother is with *him*.

"What . . . What are you actually trying to say?"

"That teenagers are selfish creatures." Ted is still smiling. "And that's why we have to make it personal. It wasn't good that Eight B was attacked, but it'll help him. He has to learn that his behavior has consequences. In real life, his actions destroyed others, but here he'll suffer the consequences of those actions himself. That's what makes No Exit so unique."

The way Ted talks about it—as if he really thinks this is a good thing!

"I can't force you to believe in it, Twenty-Five A, but I hope there will come a time when you realize that No Exit is the best thing that could have happened to you."

Come on. Come on, you bitch.

"That will never happen."

Ted spreads his hands. "Who knows?"

"May I have my urn back?" My eyes are fixed on Mom.

"I'll keep it with me for now." Ted moves the urn out of view.

I take a step forward and grab the edges of the screen, as if I might be able to climb right into it. "Why?" I shout.

"Because I want to make sure that you're not a danger." Ted keeps looking straight at me. "We've seen your type before. Ones who think they're above the system. But that's not how it works. You are and you will remain a number. We're in charge here, Twenty-Five A. Always."

"You hit Jumper with a garbage bin?" Gwen has been silent throughout the entire story, and when I stop talking, that's the first thing she says.

"I had to do something, didn't I?"

"A garbage bin!" Gwen bursts out laughing, rolling across my mattress and bumping into me. I find myself laughing, too. I can't help it. Gwen has a grunting laugh that's kind of embarrassing but also infectious.

"He must have such a headache," says Gwen, hiccupping. "No frozen peas are going to help with that."

When we've finally stopped laughing, my stomach hurts.

"I didn't know I could still do it," Gwen says, panting. "Laugh like that, I mean. After . . ."

Silence. I know exactly what she wanted to say. When someone passes, there's a life before and after. And only people who know the "after" can understand that.

"Rixt used to laugh so loud that she peed her pants. Literally, I mean. She'd have this big wet patch on her jeans. She said there was nothing she could do about it."

"Mom used to laugh so loud that I was ashamed of her." I remember those moments at the shopping mall. "Her laugh boomed through the entire store and everyone looked."

Gwen nods. "And now you wouldn't give a damn."

"Exactly."

"We have to get that urn back," says Gwen. "It's just not right that she's with Ted now."

"No."

I feel nauseous again. The thought of Mom being with that creep in his office . . .

"Why does he only ever speak to us through a screen?" Gwen wonders out loud.

"Maybe he's not even on board," I say. "Or maybe he's scared of us."

Gwen smiles. "That'll be it."

She pulls her legs up and sits cross-legged.

"What do you miss most about your mom?"

"Her arms," I say without even thinking. "She could wrap them around you like she was holding the entire world. What about you? What do you miss most about Rixt?"

"Her practical side. Even when she was crying because someone had said something nasty yet again, she could still put it into perspective."

"Do people say a lot of nasty stuff, then?"

"Yeah, sure." Gwen smiles. "They talk about me on the street. They think I don't hear it, like I'm deaf as well as blind."

"What do your friends do when something like that happens?"

"I don't have any since I've been blind," Gwen says bluntly. "Rixt was my only friend."

"Your only friend?" I ask in astonishment. Jonah was right: Gwen is nice. How could someone like her have no friends?

"People are always really nice to start with." Gwen's smile fades. "But it soon changes from who *gets to* help me to who *has to* help me."

"Really?"

"The friends I had when I went blind asked me to go

to the pool one day. Mom said it wasn't safe, but I insisted. And I had five friends with me, so I thought it'd be okay. At some point, they had to go pee, and they said they'd be right back. But they didn't come back. I waited by the slides for more than forty-five minutes and then I went home."

I can see Gwen standing there with those darting eyes of hers.

How could anyone do such a thing?

"No one has ever whacked anyone with a garbage bin for me," Gwen adds.

I smile. "I'd do it in a heartbeat."

"Thanks." Gwen runs a finger over the number on her uniform. I've noticed that she does it often, as if she still can't believe she's here.

"So, how *did* you end up here?" I wonder out loud. "If you're innocent?"

Gwen blushes a little. "Maybe my mom and dad just wanted to get rid of me. I've been kind of . . . annoying recently. Everything revolves around me: I was blind, I'd lost my best friend, I was feeling sorry for myself."

"But that's not a reason to send you *here*, is it?"

"So why did your dad send you, then?"

It's like a boomerang coming back at top speed. Maybe Gwen's right.

Maybe Dad sent me away because I was annoying, too.

I'd lost my mom, I was having a hard time, I was feeling sorry for myself.

Maybe he thought my grieving and whining about Mom was irritating. Maybe he wanted to grieve in his own way: by gambling and forgetting about everything.

"How was Rixt killed?" I say, quickly changing the subject.

Gwen blushes deep red, and I immediately regret my question.

"If you want to tell me, that is."

"Not yet," says Gwen, rubbing her number again. "But I will."

"You hit him on the head with a garbage bin?" Jonah looks at me with wide eyes.

"But you knew that, didn't you? You were there!"

"I had my head in the toilet, remember?" Jonah has a stack of playing cards in his hands, and he's shuffling them over and over. He hasn't eaten a bite of the spaghetti in front of him.

He glances over at a spot a few tables away.

I follow his gaze and see that Jumper is the center of attention again. That guy's like a barbecue that everyone wants to stand around.

"He's not going to do anything else to you," I say. "Tina said that herself."

"He's still my cellmate," says Jonah. "As long as that's the case, I'm not going to sleep."

"Hey, why is he called Jumper?" I remember Jumper's comment after 4B's death. He said something ominous about his name.

"That's what he calls himself. He drove someone to suicide." Jonah turns over the top card. A jack of diamonds falls onto the table. He returns it to the pack.

"What?"

Jonah looks up. "It was a boy named Romeo. Jumper bullied him until he jumped off a high bridge. Straight into the water. The boy drowned."

My stomach flips, and Gwen slowly lowers her fork.

"Th-that's awful," I stammer.

"Jumper is rotten to the core," says Jonah. He finally puts down the playing cards. "You guys weren't there. He looked so . . . proud. What kind of person calls themselves Jumper after . . ."

"You need to get out of cabin eight," I say. "As soon as possible."

"How do you plan to make that happen?" Jonah looks over at Tina, who's standing in a corner of the restaurant. "You going to ask her?"

"Why not?"

"I can think of a thousand reasons why not," says Jonah.

"And I can think of one good reason why." I slide my chair out. "Back in a moment."

Tina looks at me in surprise.

"What do you want?" she asks.

"Jonah has to leave cabin eight." I glance at Jumper, who apparently just said something amusing, because the whole table bursts out laughing. "Eight A is a psychopath."

Tina frowns. "Eight A has been punished for his action. He won't attack Eight B again."

"Jumper made a guy commit suicide," I say. "Jonah has to get out of there."

Tina looks over at Jumper's table. She has to understand that I'm right, that Jonah's in danger.

But then she turns back to me and shakes her head.

"You will remain in the cabins assigned to you. Eight B will have to fend for himself."

3. A STORM ON THE WAY

DIARY OF ~~━━━━━~~

Why hasn't he told anyone yet?
   Instead he's just making me suffer.
   He's letting me dangle, like a fish on a hook.
   And when the moment comes, he'll cut off my head.

—

That guy is sick.

VESPER

I don't say anything when Gwen drags her mattress into my room and puts it on the floor next to my bed.

I didn't really know her early this morning, but now it feels like we can't live without each other.

It's like No Exit has a time zone all of its own. Every hour feels like a day. Or longer.

The familiar tune plays again. I already know the recorded intro by heart.

"Good evening, Bullies." Ted looks at us, as calm as ever.

I feel my body react immediately, as if I'm allergic to him. Since my private conversation with him this afternoon, that feeling has gotten even worse.

"The first night is always the hardest, but hey, you're off to a good start."

I dig my nails into my palms. How can that man say such things?

Someone is dead.

It's like it doesn't matter. As if 4B is a sacrifice, one that No Exit is happy to make.

I throw the covers over my head, but Ted's voice still gets through.

"We have a tough schedule programmed for tomorrow, so make sure to get a good rest. You're going to need all your energy."

And then the screen goes off. I'm sure I'm not going to sleep a wink. The swaying of the ship felt like a nice rocking chair before, but now all I can think is that every wave is taking us farther away from home.

Is Dad in bed now too? I bet Ollie's trying to get into his bedroom, because he usually sleeps with me.

Is Dad thinking about me? Is he missing me?

"Do you think Jumper will keep his fists to himself tonight?" Gwen says, pulling me out of my thoughts.

"No." I don't want to think about Jonah, but now I can see him before me in sharp focus. His eyes were still twinkling, but there was something else in them.

Fear?

Is that any wonder when he's sharing a cabin with someone who brags about their victims? Someone who calls himself Jumper?

Jumper should be behind bars. And I don't mean here. I mean behind real bars.

Who's going to protect Jonah if that lunatic attacks him again in the night?

Gwen takes a deep breath. "Can I ask you something?"

I know what's coming. I'm actually surprised she hasn't brought it up before.

"Why do you hate it so much when people cry?"

I don't reply. Maybe I can pretend to have fallen asleep.

"Does it have to do with your mom?"

I squeeze my eyes tightly shut.

"Vesper?"

She's never going to fall for it. She must realize that I'm not asleep.

"I'm sorry." I hear a quiet sob. "I shouldn't have asked."

I clench my jaw.

"I—I do get it. I—" More sobbing.

"Oh, just shut your mouth," I growl.

Gwen snorts in amusement. "Then tell me why."

"Crying makes no sense."

"Why not?"

"It doesn't bring anyone back. Everyone cried at Mom's funeral. No one could make it to the end of their speeches. It was so awkward."

"You think?"

"Yeah. Dad was blubbing away like some little eight-year-old kid."

"And you didn't cry?"

"No, never."

"Could that be why you're so mad? Because you couldn't cry?"

"What do you mean?"

"Because you feel guilty? You know, about your mom. Because it feels like you're not sad about her death?"

"That's bullshit."

Gwen falls silent. Her words echo inside my head.

I see The Girl again. She just went on crying, even after I told her three times to stop.

Ted knows what I did. It's in my file. The thought of that man knowing everything about us . . .

I pull the covers more tightly around me.

Ted says the first night is the worst. I know that from prison movies, too. There's always someone who cries the first night.

Because of homesickness, because of regret, because of . . .

"Gwen?"

There's no answer.

When I shine the blue light of my phone on her, I see that she's fallen asleep.

* * *

"Bullies, step away from the door!"

As soon as the door slides open, I realize that Gwen and I have overslept.

I lay awake half the night, and the rest of the time I was having nightmares about Jumper. I saw him grinning as he held Jonah underwater until Jonah stopped struggling.

I leap out of bed and land on Gwen's legs. Groaning, she sits up.

"What's going on?" the guard yells when he sees us. "Where are your uniforms?"

"We . . ." I search for the right words, but it's like my head is full of cotton candy.

"Too bad." The guard presses the button and the door slides shut. "No breakfast for you two."

Jonah doesn't have any injuries, just dark-purple rings under his eyes.

"You guys are late" is all he says. Breakfast is almost over, and he's sitting at the table with his pack of playing cards.

"We were still asleep." Gwen takes a swig of her coffee. Luckily, they let us grab some. "I'm not a morning person."

"In prison you have to be a morning person." Jonah looks at me. "What about you?"

"A morning person? Not really. You?"

"I'm always on." Jonah fans out the cards on the table. "It really irritates my mom."

In a single movement, he flips all the cards over. Pretty impressive.

"Are you some kind of magician?" I ask.

"I do my best," Jonah says with a smile. "My oldest brother taught me."

"Do you get along with your brothers?" I've always been jealous of people with brothers and sisters. Dad, Mom, and I were a perfect team, the three of us, but now that Mom's not here, I'd welcome the extra safety net.

"Used to," Jonah says, spreading out the cards, but this time the flip doesn't go so well, and he sweeps them into a pack again. "But not after No Exit. When they came back, they'd changed."

"How do you mean?"

"They were quieter." Jonah shuffles the cards a little too wildly, and a few fall onto the floor. "It was like I suddenly had two . . . shadow brothers."

"I know what you mean," says Gwen. "Rixt was a shadow at the end as well."

I think about the girl in the torn photo.

Shadow is the perfect word for what I saw.

"Rixt was her best friend," I say to Jonah.

"What happened to her?"

"She was murdered," says Gwen.

Jonah's mouth gapes a little. "That's . . ."

If he says "a bummer" now, I'm going to hurt him.

"Intense."

"Yeah, it was." Gwen takes another swig of her coffee. "I always thought I was lonely before, but without her I've found out what lonely really means."

"Having a nice little chat?" Jumper grabs a chair and sits down at our table.

"What do you want?" I ask. I look at his forehead, which still has a bandage on it.

"Just socializing," says Jumper. He looks at all three of us. "I want to know what they're going to do to us today."

"Why are you asking us?" Gwen's eyes dart back and forth.

Someone else comes to stand by us. A girl with straight, dyed-black hair. It's the girl who was crying after 4B died, her roommate, 4A.

"Your actions are going to come back on all of us." Jumper sniffs. "Ted said yesterday evening that today was going to be tough. So, what should I expect?"

"Are you asking what we did?" I say.

"Yep. That's exactly what I'm asking."

"That's none of your business."

"Isn't it?" Jumper looks around. Some other people have

come closer. 4A is resting her hands on the back of Jumper's chair.

"I think everyone would like to know. One of you already got someone killed. And I want to know what the rest of the freak club is going to bring down on our heads."

"Same," says 4A. "What did you guys do?"

"I'm innocent," says Gwen.

"Innocent?" Jumper bursts out laughing. "Man, it's like a real prison in here! Those morons in jail always claim they're innocent too!"

"Just tell us," says 4A.

"You can at least give us a clue, can't you?" Jumper insists. "How bad is it? Pantsing someone? That kind of level? Or . . ."

"I bet Twenty-Five A did something way worse," says 4A. "I just know she did."

"Don't be dumb." I'm trying to stay calm, but I can feel a storm raging inside. "Who are you anyway?"

"Amy," says the girl. "So, what did you do?"

I remember Ted taking out my file.

Before long everything I did will be out in the open.

What if today is my day for karma?

I remember 9A out on the rear deck, when the whole group suddenly turned against her. And I see the look on Jonah's face as he went on pulling the lever.

How am I going to feel when what I did gets somebody hurt? Or worse?

"And what about our 'innocent' little blind girl?" Jumper says, looking at Gwen.

"Leave her alone," says Jonah.

Jumper grins. "Oh, Eight B. Are you falling in love? A good choice. She can't see that ugly head of yours."

People laugh, Amy loudest of all.

"At least his ugly head didn't get knocked out by a garbage bin," I snap.

Jumper glares at me. "I didn't get knocked out."

"You were down for the count. For at least twenty seconds," I continue. "White as a sheet."

Jumper shoves back his chair and stands up. For a moment, I think he's going to hit me, but then he gives me a forced smile.

"Are you declaring war on me, Twenty-Five A?" Jumper looks right at me. "You know Romeo didn't live to tell the tale, right?"

The boy probably didn't stand a chance. Jumper literally bullied him to death.

I look back, straight into Jumper's steel-blue eyes.

Simmer down, Gwen would probably tell me, but that's impossible with people like Jumper.

I remember the last vacation with Mom. There was a

wasp at the campsite that kept coming for me. I waved my hand at it, like, fifteen times, but it still kept attacking me.

So there was only one thing for it. Flip-flop off—and whack it.

Jumper is just like that wasp.

"If you want war," I say, much more calmly than I feel, "then you can have it."

"What the hell did you just do?" hisses Jonah. We're alone in the cafeteria now. The others have gone to the pool. It's weird that we still get "free time" here, as if it really is some kind of luxury vacation after all.

"You declared war on Jumper!" Jonah taps his forehead. "Are you out of your mind?"

"He declared war on me," I correct him. "Did you even hear what he said?"

"So?" yells Gwen. "You should have just kept your mouth shut."

"I can't do that. Why do you think I'm in here?"

Jonah is silent. He knows exactly what I mean. He's done a thousand dumb things too.

But Gwen keeps going.

"You heard why he calls himself Jumper, right?" She closes her eyes for a moment. "He's enjoying this."

"Maybe I am too." I look at her. "Like I said: I'm here for a reason. Who says I'm not just as crazy as him?"

"I do." Gwen's eyes are on me again, even though she can't see me.

"You've only known me for a day," I say.

"That's enough," says Gwen. "I know people. You guys are not like Jumper."

"I held someone underwater until he almost drowned," says Jonah. "Everyone was laughing. Which is why I just kept on going. I think I needed the laughter."

"You regret it" is all that Gwen says. "Jumper doesn't."

Jonah doesn't reply.

"I can see that you do," Gwen says quietly. "Even without my eyesight."

"Bullies!" Tina is waiting for us at the top of the stairs. "Welcome on deck. How was your first night?"

There's some mumbling but no one really replies.

"How was your night, Eighteen A?" Tina asks a girl who's standing right at the front.

"Great," she replies.

"You sure about that?" asks Tina. "Or did you cry until about two in the morning because you were missing your mommy and daddy so much?"

The girl looks horrified.

"There's no privacy here," says Tina. "You gave up that right long ago."

A wave of whispers ripples around the group. It slowly dawns on me what Tina's saying.

"They can *hear* us," I say breathlessly to Gwen.

How is that possible? I haven't seen any microphones. Or does the screen have a listening device inside?

That means they've heard everything. All the things Gwen and I talked about. About Rixt, about Mom.

I feel dirty, like someone's been pawing at me.

That stuff was private. Really, really private.

"What about Two B?" Tina says, turning to a boy. "Does your roommate already know you don't like girls?"

I can't believe what's happening here. How *dare* Tina do such a thing?

But 2A, who's standing beside him, nods. "As a matter of fact, yes."

Tina's smile doesn't disappear. In fact, it just becomes all the sweeter.

"Isn't it amazing what No Exit does? It quickly brings you closer to what really matters. You get to know yourself so much better." Then she turns to another boy. "And how did you sleep, Thirteen B? Did you—"

"Why are we here?" Jonah shouts, drowning out her voice.

Tina looks at him, clearly annoyed. "Excuse me?"

"You made us come all the way up those dumb stairs to the top deck, but what for?"

"Eight B. You again?"

"That's right." Jonah nods. "I had a wonderful night's sleep, with my thumb in my mouth and my head on my stuffie. My other hand was inside my pajama bottoms, by the way. Just in case you were going to mention that." I hear people laughing.

I think I needed the laughter.

The only one who definitely isn't laughing is Tina. Her smile has finally disappeared.

"I expected you to take it down a notch or two after yesterday, Eight B," she says coolly.

"No way," says Jonah. "Sticking my head down the toilet just makes even more shit come out of my mouth."

There's more laughter, but I don't join in. What's Jonah trying to do?

"I fart in bed," Gwen says. "Really loud."

The whole group looks at her now. Gwen goes a bit red and rocks back and forth on her feet.

What's she up to? She's always telling me that I need to keep my cool!

"Me too," yells Jonah. "Wet ones."

"Fine," says Tina. "That's enough for today. You have one more hour of free time and then you can go back to your cabins."

Slowly, the group falls silent. I see Jonah take Gwen's hand and give it a squeeze.

Then I realize why they did that. They wanted to divert her attention before there were any more victims.

A wave of pride goes through me. Those guys are *my* friends.

No one survives prison on their own.

Gwen was right.

When Tina has left, Jumper steps forward.

"You guys see that?"

I follow his gaze and see a big white diving board jutting out above the sea from the front of the deck.

"Yeah, it's a diving board. What about it?" asks 9A.

"I think it's an exit," Jumper says with a grin. "If you can't take it any longer on board, you can always jump off."

DIARY OF ██████████

He called me a dick today.

In front of everyone.

Just to see how I'd react.

I just walked on by, but I could feel my cheeks burning. I hoped that would be the end of it, but I heard a few people laughing.

And laughter is like fuel for him.

It's what keeps him going.

He yelled after me: ████████████████████████
████████

It felt like I was breaking into a thousand pieces.
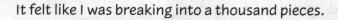

My hands are shaking as I'm writing this.

He needs to be stopped.
For good.

VESPER

"That diving board..." Jonah is as white as a sheet. "You think he was serious?"

"Of course not," I say quickly. But still I wonder. No Exit is crazy enough.

"What on earth are they thinking?" Gwen shakes her head. "There's no way I'd dare set foot on that thing."

"You won't have to," I say. "I promise you."

Gwen smiles. "Thanks."

"He's actually the one who should jump," I say, looking at Jumper. "That would be real karma."

"You think?" Jonah looks at me. "Then I should have died instead of Four B."

"That's not what I meant," I say quickly, but I could kick myself. Why did I say that?

"Can we sit with you guys?" someone says.

When I look up, I see 9A and 9B standing there.

"Sure." I move up to make room.

The boy with the little curls holds out his hand to me. "I'm Brian."

"I'm Bo." The girl shakes my hand too. She has short light-blond hair. There's something boyish about her, with her sharp jawline and her narrow build.

"Vesper, Jonah, and Gwen," I say, going around the group. "Or Twenty-Five A—"

"No numbers." Bo makes a face. "Please." I smile. I like her right away.

"I just wanted to"—Bo blushes—"I just wanted to say . . . sorry about your stuff."

"Doesn't matter," Gwen says. "It was No Exit that did it."

"That's nice of you, but still . . . Was there much damage?"

"Not too bad." Jonah grimaces. "Some books, a letter from my grandma . . ."

"A photo," says Gwen. "But I couldn't see it anyway."

"How about you?" Bo looks at me.

"An urn," I reply.

Brian's eyes widen. "A *what*?"

"The urn with my mom's ashes in it."

"Did they smash it?" Bo looks like she's about to faint.

"They stole it." I remember Ted's face as he showed it to me. Like he was enjoying the power. "It's in Ted's office."

"No way." Brian shakes his head. "That's disgusting! Have you been in there?"

"I saw him on screen. As always."

"I'm telling you, that guy is scared of us," says Bo. "He's probably afraid we're going to attack him or something."

"Or push him off the diving board," says Brian. "Which wouldn't be a bad idea, incidentally."

"Maybe one of you should jump," Jumper yells over at us. He's sitting at the edge of the pool, dangling his feet in the bright-blue water.

"Don't react," says Gwen, but her whole face is frozen.

"Preferably the redhead," Jumper continues. "Then I'll finally be rid of that whimpering in my cabin."

"He's got some nerve," whispers Brian. "What a jerk."

Jumper just keeps going. "Crying for home, for his mommy, for his brothers, for Four B . . ."

At that point, Jonah winces and his face turns deathly pale.

"At least I admit what I did," says Jumper. "I made someone commit suicide. I can even dare to say his name: Romeo. But *him*"—he points at Jonah—"he can't even bring himself to say her real name. She was called Amber."

We need to get away, but we just sit there. Jumper's verbal diarrhea goes on and on.

"You just keep on whining on about her, man!"

No one does anything. It's like we all have tape stuck over our mouths.

Jonah is the quietest of all. He doesn't look like a Labrador anymore—more like a frightened mutt.

Jumper jumps up. "Hello? Eight B, do you hear me? Just accept the fact that you're responsible for Amber's death. Man up and say, 'It was me who kill—"

All at once, my muscles are working again.

I leap to my feet and run at him.

I'm going to drown him.

I'm going to drown him with my own two hands.

"Twenty-Five A!" I hear someone shout, but I go on running.

Jumper is so stunned that he doesn't think to brace himself and, with all my strength, I shove him into the pool.

I fall in after him.

There's a tangle of arms and legs, but I manage to grab hold of him. I just want to make him stop.

How dare he say such things?

Jonah didn't kill 4B. No Exit did!

Jumper grabs my hair. He gives it a hard tug and I scream, swallowing a big mouthful of chlorinated water.

And then I feel a strong hand on my upper arm, and someone pulls me out of the pool.

I kick out wildly, but the grip doesn't weaken. In fact, it gets tighter.

"Cool it." The voice in my ear is Harrold's. When I look up, I see that Jumper has been pulled out of the water too. He looks at me with a grin.

"You . . ." I have to get to Jumper. I have to stop him.

I pull myself free and I'm about to launch myself at him again when I get tackled to the ground. Which is followed by a punch in the stomach. I curl up, gasping for breath.

"Vesper!" I hear Gwen yell. I hope she's not dumb enough to get involved.

"That kind of behavior," says Harrold, leaning over me, "will not be tolerated."

He pulls me to my feet. The pain in my stomach is unbearable. I can barely stand upright.

"Come with me."

I leave a trail of water in the long corridor. Harrold drags me along like a rag doll and opens a door. He throws me into the empty room. The walls are made of cushions.

I realize that this is an isolation cell. I'm in solitary confinement.

I jump to my feet, but Harrold has already locked the door.

He's looking at me through the square opening in the door.

"Take some time to cool down, Twenty-Five A."

"No . . . I . . ."

Without waiting to hear what I have to say, he slides the hatch shut.

"Wait!" I yell. "How long do I need to stay in here? I'm soaked through. I . . ."

There is no answer.

I bang on the door, but it hurts my hands so much that I soon give up.

Dropping down onto the cold floor, I wrap my arms around my legs.

My wet uniform is sticking to my body. I shiver.

In the dark, the swaying of the ship is much more noticeable.

I think about Jumper. Is he being punished, too? Probably not. He's going to act like he's the victim.

But he was saying the most disgusting things about Jonah.

I think about my friends. Are they okay? Now that there are only two of them, they've become an easy target for Jumper.

How could I have been so dumb as to attack Jumper?

Gwen's right. I need to learn to control myself.

Because who's going to protect her now that I'm not

there? I hope Brian and Bo will stick with Gwen and Jonah. Brian's not only friendly, he's also big and strong.

As long as he's around, Jumper won't dare to do anything.

Will he?

I shiver again.

Where's Harrold gone?

How long are they going to leave me in here?

I'm hungry and thirsty.

Feels like I've been locked up in here for hours.

"I get it! Let me out!"

I thump the door again, but there's no point.

I'm the only one who's bothered by my screaming.

An isolation cell.

When I heard people in documentaries saying that solitary confinement is hell, I always thought: *How bad can it be? A few hours on your own is over in no time, isn't it?*

But that's not how it is.

You go crazy in here. Truly crazy.

"Hello?" My throat feels raw with thirst.

I need something to drink.

They can't just leave me in here forever, can they?

*   *   *

Then I hear the familiar No Exit tune coming through the speaker.

"Welcome to No Exit. The place for you so that others will be safe."

And then silence.

What's going on?

Was that a mistake or are they finally releasing me?

It must be late in the afternoon by now.

"Vesper?"

The hatch opens, and I squeeze my eyes shut in the bright light.

Then I see that it's not Harrold. It's a girl.

Am I going crazy?

Am I seeing things?

My body is stiff with cold.

"Vesper?" the girl repeats.

"Who . . . ," I begin.

The girl's face clouds over. "You don't remember who I am, huh?"

I think frantically, but it doesn't come to me. "Should I?"

In one movement, she slides the hatch shut.

"Wait!" I dive forward and start pounding on the door again. "Come back! Please!"

Then I hear voices on the other side of the door.

"You have to talk to her, honey. You need to put this behind you." A woman is speaking to the girl, trying to persuade her.

"That's right," says a man's voice. "We came all the way here for this moment."

Are they her mom and dad?

Then the hatch opens again.

"Fine," the girl says to me. "I'll try one more time. I'm Lizzy."

Lizzy.

Somewhere inside my head, a hatch opens.

"You . . ." I see her sitting in a classroom with posters of animals on the walls.

"You sat behind me in biology."

"Exactly." Lizzy nods.

"What . . ." My thoughts are like a Rubik's Cube, all mixed up.

What's a girl from my old high school doing here?

"I've come to talk to you," says Lizzy. "Do you remember what you did to me?"

And then the words from the information folder suddenly come back to me.

Karma and . . . confrontation!

Is this the other part of the program? Do we have to come face to face with our victims?

I remember The Girl again. Crying, pleading.

But The Girl was not Lizzy.

So, what is *she* doing here?

"Are you going to say something, or . . ." Lizzy's eyes look a bit teary.

What if she bursts out crying right in front of me?

"Yeah, yeah, of course. You . . . You were at my old high school," I say quickly. "I left there just after . . ."

Just after Mom died. My grades tanked, and Dad suggested making a fresh start somewhere else.

As if a different school would help.

A school is nothing more than a bunch of bricks and glass.

It wasn't going to bring Mom back.

"I know you left." Lizzy nods. "And I'm glad. Because you destroyed me!"

I destroyed her? What? I start racking my brain.

"You don't remember," says Lizzy. Her eyes look *really* watery now.

"Yeah, I remember." I'm thinking frantically, but all I can see is The Girl. Everything else suddenly seems hazy and blurred, as if I have sharp images of that one moment and the rest of the pictures don't work.

"No, you don't. You have no idea that you called me a—"

"Drama queen!"

Suddenly I've grabbed the right picture. The moment is sharp in focus, as if I'm back in the biology room. Lizzy was sitting behind me as usual, talking to a friend about her boyfriend who'd just broken up with her. And it was a complete drama.

The teacher wasn't there yet, and Lizzy was going into great detail about the moment when her boyfriend told her he didn't want to date her anymore. Until finally I heard sobbing coming from behind me.

It feels like I'm dying, she'd said.

She actually said that.

It was as if something snapped inside me.

I spun around in my seat and yelled at her. "You are such a drama queen!" I shouted. "You really think you're going to die because some guy doesn't want you anymore? No. You're going to die because you turn everything into a damn drama." I'd said something along those lines.

People were laughing around me.

I think I needed the laughter.

Was that why I said it? Or was it because Mom was dying? Because she was really, actually dying, and this girl had said the word like it was nothing?

I kept yelling at her and didn't stop until the teacher came into the room. He sent me to the principal, and I got detention after school.

"After you called me that, everyone else did. It became my nickname," Lizzy said, looking right at me. "When I walked down the halls, there was always someone who yelled after me: *Hey, drama queen, you going to die again?"*

Lizzy takes a deep breath. "They sprayed a crown and other stuff on my locker and edited photos of me to make me look dead, with my eyes closed and a crucifix."

"Sorry . . ."

"And when I got mad, they just laughed even more. Because I always cry when I get mad." Lizzy wipes her eyes on the back of her hand. "Thanks to you, I was bullied all of a sudden."

"Sorry," I say again. "I had no idea."

"Of course you didn't." A woman comes to stand in front of the hatch. She looks exactly like Lizzy, but older. "You bullies leave behind a trail of destruction. Which is why we're so pleased with the No Exit program. Aren't we, Liz?"

Lizzy nods.

"What's going to happen to this bully now?" I hear the mother ask.

"She's midway through her journey." Tina's voice. "She'll be a different person when she sets foot on dry land again."

"Or go back in a body bag," I say.

There's a silence.

"Oh, you didn't know?" I look at Lizzy's mother. "One bully already died."

"Twenty-Five A." Tina's voice sounds threatening. But I

don't care anymore. Maybe I did leave a trail of destruction in my wake, but No Exit is no better.

"I'm sorry, Lizzy," I say again. "I'm sorry for what I did to you. But what's happening here is not okay. They're abusing people. They're killing them!"

"All right." Tina pushes Lizzy out of the way and gives me a cold stare. "That's enough, Twenty-Five A."

She slides the hatch shut.

"Someone died!" I scream. "No Exit isn't a reeducation program. They kill bullies!"

I slam on the door three times, but the dull thumps confirm what I already suspected: no one can hear me.

I'm alone again.
Really alone.
I think this is the definition of loneliness.
All alone in the world.
Cold and wet.
Frozen.
Broken.

"Twenty-Five A." The door swings open and the bright light makes me squint.

"You're done," says the guard. "You can go back to the group."

"Vesper!" It's Jonah.

Even before I've taken the last step to the upper deck, Gwen throws her arms around me. I mumble into her hair that I'm thirsty.

Jonah fetches a bottle of water, which I down in one gulp.

Gwen brings some blankets and wraps them around me. Her arm around my shoulders feels warmest of all.

It's pitch-black outside. It must be evening. Was I in that cell all day?

"What time is it?"

"Eleven," says Gwen. "We were allowed to stay up late. It's been a . . . tough day. But everyone is still here."

Stay up late, as if this is some kind of kids' party.

"What happened to you?" Gwen rubs my arms, trying to warm me up. Jonah looks at me with a worried expression.

"I was in solitary confinement."

Gwen and Jonah look shocked.

"Seriously? They have an isolation cell?" Disgust is dripping from Jonah's face.

"You bet." I know it's going to give me nightmares tonight. Being back in that place, cold and lonely.

"And I think I made No Exit even more mad."

"Why?" Gwen looks shocked. "What did you do?"

I feel ashamed.

Why can't I control myself? I need to make sure the three of us stay together. It's the only way we're going to get through these ten days alive.

"I couldn't help it. Lizzy's parents were saying how good the program is. So I told them that No Exit murders people. What else was I supposed to do?"

"Huh? Who's Lizzy?"

I hesitate. Do I really want Gwen and Jonah to know about this part of me? But I can't go back now.

As I tell them, Gwen's face becomes paler and paler. The only part I leave out is the bit about not recognizing Lizzy. I can't bring myself to say that.

"The confrontation phase?" Jonah says slowly. "So does that mean all the victims are on the ship?"

I nod. I hadn't even thought about that.

"In a separate section, I think."

"The place for them so that they will be safe," Gwen says, imitating the recorded voice.

Jonah nods. "I saw a sign somewhere saying ACCESS FORBIDDEN BEYOND THIS POINT. It must be there."

"Did Jumper behave while I was away?" I ask.

Jonah nods. "By his standards, yes, but I think they're planning something."

"What do you mean?"

"Him and his friends." Jonah makes a face. "That Amy is seriously disturbed too. She pushed Gwen over at lunch and just stood there laughing at her."

I feel my hands tingling. "And let me guess: no one saw anything, right?"

"Well, I certainly didn't," Gwen says dryly.

Jonah bursts out laughing. "I think we're safe as long as Brian is around. That guy's like a grizzly bear."

"Sure is," I agree. "Then we need to make sure that Brian and Bo stay on our side."

"They hate Jumper just as much as we do, so I think we're good." Jonah looks at me. "I'm glad you're back, Ves."

People often shorten my name, but it's like I'm hearing it for the first time.

Then Jonah lets out a deep sigh and leans back on the sun lounger. Gwen and I do the same. I look up at the vast ocean of stars above us.

"In a different situation, that view would be amazing," I say.

"What are we looking at?" Gwen says.

"A thousand little white dots," I reply, taking her hand. "There." I point with her finger. "That's the Little Dipper."

"And what else?"

"That's it," I say. "I don't know the other constellations."

We look up at the sky for a while. It feels strange to see the stars. It gives me a misplaced sense of freedom.

As if I could travel anywhere through those glowing dots.

"What was it like? Seeing Lizzy?" Jonah suddenly asks.

I know he's thinking about his own victim. Are they on board too?

"I was expecting someone else," I answer honestly. "Lizzy wasn't the worst."

"Then who was?"

"I never say her name," I reply. "I always call her The Girl."

Jonah nods, as if he understands. "And she was the worst?"

"Yeah."

I try to push the images away, but they keep coming back, like some kind of stalker.

"What about you?" I hear Gwen ask.

"One of my victims was named Bruno," says Jonah. "He was in the sixth grade, and he had this huge backpack. It was way too big for him. With a loop on top, which I used to grab when he was walking in front of me. I said I was taking my backpack poodle for a walk."

I can't help laughing.

"Sorry," I say, but Jonah nods.

"Yeah, it was kind of funny. But obviously not for Bruno."

"No."

"And when that joke got old, I had to come up with something new." Jonah pauses. "And then my brother thought of an idea. At school we had this staircase with these wooden ball things on the handrail at the points where it turned the corners. He said the loop on Bruno's backpack would probably fit over it perfectly."

"No . . . ," I say quietly.

"Oh, yes." Jonah stares up at the sky. "My brother and I lifted this kid over the rail. Bruno was squealing like a stuck pig. Must have thought we wanted to throw him from two stories up."

I can picture it. Bruno with his big backpack and those other two boys, who were so much bigger and stronger.

"We hung the loop over the ball and left him hanging." Jonah's jaw twitches. "Half the school stood below and watched him scream. And no one did anything. Not even when the loop began to tear."

"Did he fall?" I hear myself asking breathlessly.

"No. The janitor pushed us out of the way and pulled Bruno back up. The week after that, my brother was sent on a *vacation for young people*."

"And you weren't?"

"Matt took the blame. Leon had done the same for him before."

Jonah's big brothers.

I try to imagine it, each of them disappearing one by one and coming back as ghosts of their former selves.

"Did no one ever warn you to stop bullying people?"

"Of course they did. But when I asked them why, they didn't answer. And I don't do things without a reason."

"They must love you at school," I say, repeating what he'd said to me on the first day.

"Oh, sure." Jonah makes a face. "I was warned by two brothers, but I still messed up."

He's still looking straight up at the sky.

"Are you scared that Bruno's on board now?"

"Yeah," says Jonah. "Or maybe they've found Esther. Or Amélie or Samir or . . ."

"Do you still remember all your victims by name?"

Jonah turns to look at me. "Don't you?"

I slipped up! I pretend to take a swig of water, but my bottle's empty.

"You serious?" Jonah shakes his head. "You didn't recognize Lizzy?"

"Okay, I'm a terrible person." I squeeze the plastic bottle. "I had no idea who she was at first."

No one says anything. The only sound comes from the waves crashing against the bow of the ship.

"Now who's the drama queen?" Gwen has hardly said

anything throughout the entire conversation, but now she spits out the words and stands up. "You guys decided to bully those people all on your own, didn't you? You didn't bully them for someone else."

I slowly shake my head. "No, no one made me do it."

"So the two of you need to take some responsibility and stop acting so pathetic and sorry for yourselves!" She stands up and walks away.

I watch, stunned, as she finds her way to the stairs and disappears.

Jonah whistles. "Whoa, she was really mad."

I nod as Gwen's words slowly sink in. "But she's right. We've brought this on ourselves. And she's innocent."

DIARY OF █████

Did I ever tell you I used to ███████

The thought of him telling *everyone* that I'm a ███
That can't happen.
That mustn't happen.

Hang in there.

VESPER

"Bullies, step away from the door!"

Day three begins exactly like the day before, but Gwen and I are ready this time.

My stomach's rumbling like crazy. I didn't get any food yesterday because of my time in the cell.

Gwen rubs the number on her chest. She's barely said anything since yesterday evening. When I came back from the deck at eleven-thirty, she was already in bed.

Her mattress was still next to my bed, but that was it. She lay there with her back to me and said nothing.

I thought about her words half the night. She's right: Jonah and I didn't have to be bullies. We chose to do it by ourselves.

I wanted to tell her that, but now that I know No Exit is listening in . . .

"Follow me," the guard says when everyone's lined up in the corridor.

"Where are we going?" I wonder out loud. "The restaurant's the other way."

"Breakfast is later today," the guard says.

I curse to myself. Nothing to eat again?

What's going to happen now? Where are they taking us?

I look back. Jonah is walking some distance behind us. I see Jumper trying to trip him up, but like yesterday with Amy, the guards apparently don't notice.

The guard leads us into a big room with rings hanging from the ceiling, mats against the walls, and a basket at either end. A gym.

Are we going to play some kind of game?

I don't know if I can do it without breakfast.

I hate sports of all kinds anyways. The only thing I like doing is taking Ollie for walks, particularly when Mom was still alive. We could talk for hours as Ollie chased his ball on the beach.

The memory hurts. It always does.

Too much pain.

I quickly shake it off.

"Bullies!" Tina comes into the room. "We're here to get a great start to the day. How many of you like to do sports?"

A few cautious hands go up, including Jumper's. I'm

not surprised. He might not be as wide as Brian, but he's muscly.

It's a miracle that he didn't drown me in the pool yesterday. I read somewhere that anger makes a person stronger. That angry people are capable of doing things they'd never have thought possible.

But now that my anger has calmed down, the fear is coming back.

Jonah thinks Jumper is planning something.

"I'm pleased to hear it," says Tina. "Research has shown that a lot of bullying is the result of a lack of exercise. Doing sports can be a good way to let out anger, frustration—"

"Then those researchers didn't take Jumper into account," Jonah says quietly into my ear. He's standing behind me, and I can feel his warm breath on my neck. "I don't think working out every day would change him at all."

"Neither do I." I turn to look at Jonah and see the dark bags under his eyes. "Did you manage to get some sleep?"

"A bit," Jonah says. "Until they came and woke me."

"What for?" I ask.

"My confrontation phase." Jonah's face clouds over. "I don't know what's worse: confrontation or karma."

"Was it Bruno?" I ask, remembering the story about the big backpack.

Jonah nods. "Bruno's a big guy now, pushing six feet."

"What did he say?"

"Not much. Mainly stared. That was even scarier. They left us on our own for fifteen minutes and I was scared the whole time that he was going to attack me. But he didn't. Seems he's not as much of a shit as I am."

"Eight B and Twenty-Five A, please focus!" Tina says, looking at us. "We're going to start with a warm-up: three laps of the room."

There's sighing and groaning.

I look around. I only notice now just how many guards there are. There are eight of them lined up around the walls.

"Think they're scared we're going to escape?"

"Yeah, I bet." Jonah follows my gaze. "Why else would they—"

At that moment, all the lights go off. It's pitch-dark; for a moment, I think I'm back in the isolation cell.

"What's going on?" someone shouts.

"Hello?"

"Tina?"

There's no answer.

I feel a hand on my arm and sharp nails in my skin.

"Vesper," I hear Gwen say. "I have to—"

"Stay with me," I say firmly. "Jonah?"

"I'm here," he replies. "We'll stay togeth—"

"Aaaaaaah!" A loud cry cuts through the darkness. Followed by a high-pitched shriek.

What's going on?

I spin toward where the sound came from, but there's no point. I can't see a thing.

Then someone else screams.

"Hey!" someone yells. "What's happening?"

Another scream.

"No. Don't! Please!" The voice sounds panicky—and very close. I hear dull thuds and more screaming.

"Jumper, help!" That was Amy.

"We have to get out of here," yells Jonah. "Now!"

I'm about to say to Gwen that she should lead us when I notice she's not holding my arm anymore.

"Gwen!"

Why did she let go of me? Is she in danger?

Someone slams into me, and there's a shove in my back. There's more yelling and screaming, and people start running.

Someone is crying, but I barely register it. Because I suddenly realize what all those guards were doing here, and what's happening now.

The guards are attacking us.

DIARY OF ███████

███████

Tell me the world's not as rotten as it seems.

—

Think about fun things.
    Think about extra-big scoops of ice cream.
    Or a short line at the roller coaster.
    Think about the summer ███████
███████
███████
███████
███████
███

4. SOS

VESPER

"Gwen!" My voice is lost in the screaming all around me. It's pitch-dark. I drag Jonah through a tangle of arms and legs.

We need to get out of here, but where's the exit?

And then I bump into a wall. The mat under my hands feels cool.

This was close to the door, wasn't it?

"Jonah, this way. Jonah?" I feel his hand slip out of mine, and I hear a heartrending cry.

"Vesper!"

"Jonah!" I reach out around me, searching for his hand, an arm, a leg, but there's nothing.

Where is he?

Did they get him?

I fall onto my hands and knees and feel around on the floor. There's a shoe, laces, pants . . . Is that Jonah?

But then I hear a voice, very close.

"Hello, Twenty-Five A."

It's Harrold.

"Please," I beg. "Please, I—"

And then I go down.

My head is pounding like mad when I open my eyes.

It takes a while to dawn on me, but then I know where I am. The gym.

The lights are back on.

Jonah.

Where's Jonah?

When I lift my head, I feel pain shoot through it. I groan.

Next to me is Amy, gazing up at the ceiling. She's blinking really fast, like she can hardly believe where she is.

I try to stand up, but I can't. My legs are like lead, and when I look down, I see why.

Someone is lying on me, pressing my legs to the floor with all his weight.

"Hey," I manage to say. "Get off."

I push at his arm, but I can't make him move.

"H-help," I croak. Not a good idea—another stabbing pain shoots through my head.

Around me, I see people standing up.

Where on earth is Jonah?

And Gwen?

She was suddenly gone. Why did she let go of my arm? Did she get hit by a guard, like I did?

"Help me," I say to Amy, who's scrambling to her feet. "Someone's lying on me."

Amy doesn't react, just stumbles away.

What should I do?

I give the body another shove, but it doesn't budge an inch.

"Get. Off. Me." I try to kick the body off my legs.

Why won't he wake up?

"Vesper..." When I look up, I see Jonah standing there. There's blood trickling down his forehead and over his cheek, but he sounds okay.

"I'll help you."

Jonah grabs the dark-blue uniform with two hands and pulls. It doesn't work at first, but when I help him, we turn the body over in one movement. The dull thud as the body hits the ground echoes through the room.

"Come on." Jonah grabs my hand and pulls me up.

My head is thumping, everything is spinning, but I'm on my feet.

I throw my arms around him and hold him tight.

"So...," says Jonah.

"Don't you dare," I hiss in his ear. "Don't you dare say something stupid."

"I wouldn't dare." Jonah puts his arms around my waist, and we stand there for a moment.

All around us, I see dark-blue uniforms walking toward one another. Some are hugging, like Jonah and me. Others are sitting together on the floor.

"No!" A loud scream startles us. I immediately let go of Jonah and look at Bo, who's pointing a trembling finger in our direction.

What's wrong?

Is Jonah more badly wounded than I thought?

Two guards rush past us. I see them bending down and grabbing the body that Jonah and I just moved. They pick him up.

It's Brian.

I didn't even look at him for a second. I just shoved him off of me like a sack of garbage.

Bo is crying. "Brian . . ."

"He's still alive," I hear a guard say. "We'll take him to the infirmary."

"Where's Gwen?"

Jonah shrugs. He takes a swig from the bottle of water that the guards gave us.

We're all sitting in the middle of the room.

Bo is with us, staring ahead in a daze. There are all kinds

of things I'd like to say to her, but I wouldn't know where to begin.

If it had been Jonah, I wouldn't want anyone trying to comfort me either.

A nurse helps Jumper with his bleeding lip. No Exit has a hard-core medical team on board. It makes me want to puke.

They knew there would be serious injuries today, so the medics were probably on high alert.

"Twenty-Five A?" A medic crouches beside me. "Okay if I take a look at your head wound?"

My blood is boiling. "What do *you* think?"

"I think it'd be a good idea if I just—"

"Do you know what I think would be a good idea?" I look him in the face. "I think it'd be a good idea if you guys let us go home."

The man acts like he didn't hear me and reaches out his hand.

"Do not touch me!"

"I just need to—"

"Screw you!" If he comes any closer, I'm going to bite him. So what if I have to go back into isolation?

"You sure?" he asks.

"Why do you work here?" I ask him. "Why would you want to be part of—"

I look around the room. There are injured people

everywhere, some worse off than others. 20B is covered in blood. Looks like her eyebrow got torn.

"— this?"

The man smiles. His smile is just like Tina's.

Maybe you need a smile like that to work here.

"I believe in No Exit," he says.

"Why?"

"Because it works. All the evidence is there."

"Did you get bullied when you were younger?"

The man's smile disappears.

"I'll take that as a yes," I say. "And does this make your past better?"

The man doesn't say anything.

"An eye for an eye," I say. "Is that the solution?"

"It works," the man says. "The bullies who leave the ship never bully anyone again. One day you'll believe in No Exit too."

"I will not," I say firmly. "Never."

"You will." The man stands up. "Believe me."

Then he goes to the next injured person.

"Well done," says Jonah. "You didn't even try to drown him in the pool."

I smile. "I wanted to."

Then I look around again. "Where on earth is Gwen?"

"She must have gotten away."

"You think?" I look at the doors. Is that how she escaped?

She's an expert at moving around in the dark, of course. It doesn't make any difference to her if the lights are on or off.

The medics have finished their work. They quickly leave the room, along with the guards.

Harrold stays behind on his own, standing in front of the door.

Jumper stands up. His lip has stopped bleeding.

"Okay. Whose karma was this?"

Is he going on about that again? What difference does it make?

Jumper walks around the group. Although only three people are missing, it feels as if our numbers have thinned out considerably.

"Well?" He looks at 20B. Her face has been cleaned. There's a stitch in her eyebrow. "Yours, is it? You ever attack anyone in the dark?"

"No."

"Whose is it, then?" Jumper looks at Bo. "How about you?"

When Bo doesn't respond, he jabs her in the side with his sneaker.

"Well?"

"Leave her alone. They took her friend," says Jonah. "Besides, we already went through Bo's karma phase."

"Well?" Jumper looks around the rest of the group. "Anyone going to confess?"

"Maybe this was Four B's karma," someone says.

"Could be," says Jumper. "Then it's a good thing she's dead."

"You can't do this," I hear Jonah say.

"Can't I?" Jumper takes a step forward. "And why not?"

I can see Jonah's eyes changing. The silence is deafening. I'm afraid that he's about to attack Jumper. He can't be that dumb, can he?

"Whoever's karma it is, it's a cowardly thing to do," someone says, breaking the silence. "Don't you think?"

"Everything we've done is cowardly," says Jonah, tearing his eyes away from Jumper. "That's why we're here."

Jumper sniffs. "We're here because we were screwed over by our parents. And by our schools."

"They didn't do it just for no reason, did they?" Jonah's face is red. "We made mistakes."

"You call it mistakes. I call it justice."

Jonah shakes his head. "Someone committed suicide because of you. You call that justice?"

Jumper jabs his finger at Jonah. "You have no idea, Eight B. The world is a better place without Romeo."

"So, what did he do?" Jonah's cheeks are getting redder and redder. "Was he overweight? Nose too big? Red hair? Was he gay?"

"Romeo was just . . . disgusting. He was asking for it."

"Bet you're one of those bullies who were bullied themselves," Jonah snaps at him. "A walking cliché."

Patches of red appear on Jumper's neck. He sweeps his long bangs off his face, but they immediately fall back over his eyes.

"Look out, Eight B." Jumper's voice suddenly sounds a couple octaves lower. The whole gym seems to vibrate. "Or you'll end up like Romeo."

Then there's the sound of the familiar tune.

"No Exit. The place for you so that others will be safe."

The words feel more and more like an ice-cold bath.

Then Ted's voice booms around the room.

"Bullies. One of you attacked someone in the dark. And as you know, karma always comes back to haunt you here. So, who do you have to thank for this one? That would be . . . Four B."

"Told you so," the girl says.

"Where's Brian?" Bo yells at the speakers. "I mean Nine B. Is . . . Is he okay?"

Ted doesn't seem to hear her. Maybe he's deliberately ignoring her question.

"And Gwen?" I shout. "Where is she?"

"She was the only one to get away in time." Luckily, Ted does answer my question. The answer makes all the tension flow from my body. Gwen is all right. She's still alive.

"Being blind has its advantages, right?"

* * *

"Help yourselves," Tina says, pointing at the breakfast buffet. But I only have eyes for Gwen. She's sitting at our table, waiting for us.

"Gwen!" I throw my arms around her and hug her as tightly as I did Jonah. "Where were you?"

"Are you guys . . ." Gwen holds me at arm's length, her eyes seeming to scan my face. "Are you hurt? Where's Jonah? Is everything okay?"

"Everything's fine," I say quickly. "Not with Brian, though. They took him away."

"Is he dead?" Gwen's face is deathly pale.

"No, but he's injured."

I look at Bo, who has come to sit across from us. She doesn't have a tray.

"Bo," I say. "It's going to be okay. You'll see."

"How do you know that?" Bo looks at me. "This is No Exit."

"I should have helped you guys." Gwen sighs. "I'm the only one who could see as well as I usually can."

"You couldn't have helped," I say. "It was complete chaos. Those guards attacked us like wild animals."

"Did they . . ." Gwen gulps. "Did they have weapons?"

"Batons, I think." I reach up to touch my head.

"They must have had night-vision goggles," says Jonah.

He has a tray of food in front of him, which he places in the middle of the table so that everyone can help themselves. "They knew exactly where we were, so they had the advantage."

"Night vision." I repeat slowly. "That is seriously disturbed."

"Yep." Jonah takes a swig of orange juice.

"I can't believe that was what Four B did to someone." I look at Gwen. "They said it was Four B's karma."

"Really?" Gwen is still pale. "That's terrible. I'm so sorry I left the room."

"Hey," Jonah says, leaning across the table to take her hand. "Of course you had to get out of there as quickly as you could. Vesper and I would have done the same. If it hadn't been so damn dark in there, that is."

"*No Exit. The place for you so that others will be safe.*"

The tune slowly dies away, and Ted appears on the big screen in the restaurant.

I slowly lower my knife and fork. Because in the background in his office, I can see . . .

"Th-the urn," I stammer.

Jonah quietly curses. "What an incredible . . ."

"He's doing it on purpose," I say. "He *knows* I can see it."

The urn is so close, somewhere on this ship, but at the

same time Mom feels farther away than ever. Ted knows I'll never be able to get to the urn.

"Bullies." Ted says with a smile. "You have the rest of the day off. You've earned it after this morning. If there's any damage remaining, the medical team is here to help you."

How dare he? How can he talk about it so casually? Like what just happened in the gym was normal?

"Damage?" Jumper can't hold back any longer. He shoves his plate away. "Come here, and I'll give you some damage."

Ted just goes on talking. "Enjoy everything that the ship has to offer. Take a dip in our heated pool, try your luck in our casino—"

"How about it?" yells Jumper.

I see Tina exchange a look with the guard. This is about to get out of hand.

"Or spend the day on our deck. The weather's beautiful."

I can't believe what's coming out of Ted's mouth. Brian is suffering somewhere on this ship. Or maybe he's already dead.

Bo was right. We have no idea how Brian is doing now.

He felt so heavy when he was lying on top of me. He felt dead.

I glance at Bo, who still hasn't eaten a bite.

"We hope you realize that we're doing this for your own good. No Exit is here for *you*," Ted continues.

"Don't make me laugh, man." Now Jumper jumps to his feet. "Do you really believe that?"

"Results in the past have shown that—"

"Bullshit! You're killing us!" Jumper spits out the words. "Attacking a bunch of unarmed kids in the dark. Yeah, that's really brave!"

Ted falls silent. I glance at the urn in the background. Am I ever going to get it back?

I hate Jumper, but for the first time I hope he'll go a step further. Ted deserves everything that Jumper is saying.

"No clever words now?" Jumper continues. "You're the biggest coward of all. You're pathetic. Acting all tough on the other side of a camera. Why don't you come here! I'll destroy you. You'll beg for mercy. I promise you."

Everyone in the room is holding their breath. The corners of Ted's mouth are twitching. His piercing eyes are staring into the camera.

Is he going to do it? Is he finally going to come out here?

But then Ted smiles. In a calm and controlled voice, he says, "Like I said: enjoy the ship."

And then the screen goes black.

"Okay, I'm going gambling," Jonah says, pushing back his chair. "I've still got one last fifty left. Who's coming?"

I look up. Gambling? Again?

"Me," Gwen says immediately.

"Me too." To my surprise, even Bo stands up.

"What about you?" Jonah looks at me expectantly. The cut on his forehead makes him look kind of wild.

"Are you falling for those slot machines again?" I ask. "You know you're going to lose it all."

"We've already lost everything" is all that Jonah says. "Can't you see that?"

The four of us head to a machine with pyramids and scarab beetles on the reels. The flashing letters say that the game is called *The Mummy's Curse*. I look at the white sticker on the top right of the machine.

HOW MUCH IS GAMBLING COSTING YOU? MAKE SURE YOU STOP IN TIME, it says.

It makes no sense. No one ever looks at the words. It's the same with smoking. The warnings on the packets have no impact. If you want to smoke, then you'll smoke. If you want to gamble, you'll gamble.

Dad's living proof of that.

Jonah gives his money a kiss and slides it into the machine.

The volume rises; the lights start flashing.

"It sounds so exciting," Gwen says.

"They do it on purpose," I reply. "So you become addicted."

"Don't spoil my brief moment of happiness, Vesper." Jonah leans over the machine. The first three rounds go badly, the amount decreasing quickly.

"You see, this—" I say, but then the machine suddenly starts singing.

"A bonus game!" Jonah's eyes are sparkling.

"Can I have a go?" asks Bo.

"Sure." Jonah takes a big step aside to let her in. "Go ahead."

Then he gives me a wink.

And that's when I understand why we're here. It's not for Jonah, not because he's so eager to get back to gambling. It's so we can help Bo forget for a moment how worried she is about Brian.

And the worst part is: it's working.

It's like I'm not looking at Bo, but my dad. He was just as good at escaping into those happy little jingles.

Bo stares at the buttons. "What do I have to do?"

"Press that button on the right, and let's see what happens."

Bo looks intently at the screen. The reels spin and then . . .

"Jackpot!" Jonah holds up his hand and gives Bo a high five. "You're my lucky mascot!"

For the first time since the attack, I see Bo smile.

Jonah does a ridiculous happy dance, jumping wildly up and down.

No one cares that five minutes later the amount has halved and ten minutes later it's at zero.

"Aww, lost everything?"

Jumper's voice brings me straight back to the ship. I spin around and see that he's not alone. There's a big group around him, including Amy.

Where did they suddenly appear from? I didn't hear them coming.

"What are you guys doing here?" I ask.

They approach menacingly.

Of course, now that Brian's in the infirmary, we're an easy target.

The four of us aren't physically strong enough to . . .

"How about something a bit more exciting than that dumb slot machine?" asks Jumper.

"Like what?" Jonah says, looking at him. "Russian roulette?"

Jumper grins. "I was actually thinking about walking the plank."

The hairs on the back of my neck stand on end. Somehow Jonah had managed to make me forget where we were for a moment. As if No Exit didn't exist.

But now the reality is hitting me. Hard. "None of us are going to jump. No way," I say.

"That's not what I'm saying." Jumper looks at me, his expression ice-cold. "One of us needs to go stand on it."

I remember the huge, long plank. "Why would we want to do that?"

"Because it's exciting." Jumper grins. "Right?"

"So, one of us has to walk the plank?" Jonah says. "And just stand on it?"

"Exactly," says Amy. "And we're going to make it interesting. Risky."

"How?" asks Jonah.

"We'll all pick a card. There are fifty-two cards in a pack, so there are enough for everyone."

"And then?" I don't really want to hear the rest.

"Whoever picks the lowest card has to stand on the diving board for a minute." Jumper sniffs. "Ace is high, two is low."

"But there are four twos," says Jonah. "One for each suit."

"So, we'll take three of them out. Then we'll have forty-nine cards. Exactly enough for all of us. Brian can have his card when he's conscious again."

I see the look of pain on Bo's face.

It's insane. Only a sick person like Jumper could come up with an idea like this.

Amy takes out a pack of playing cards. "Here are the three twos." She throws away the two of clubs, spades, and diamonds. Then she holds up the two of hearts.

"Whoever picks this card... is going to walk the plank."

"I refuse to take part," I say immediately.

"Me too," says Bo.

"And what about you, Eight B?" Jumper looks at Jonah. "Dare to try your luck?"

I see the sparkle in Jonah's eyes. There's no way he's going to do this. Is there?

"I'm in."

"What?" I grab Jonah's arm. "Are you out of your mind?"

"Tonight," he says to Jumper. "We'll meet on deck at nine-thirty, and we'll all pick a card. Whoever gets the two of hearts will walk the plank."

"No..." I feel my stomach flip.

"We won't let him win," says Jonah. Then he leans in to me and whispers, "Trust me."

Trust him? I want to lash out at him, but then Jumper nods.

"Nine-thirty on the foredeck."

DIARY OF ~~━━━━━~~

Today on the school trip he finally did what I've been afraid of all this time.

    I can't even write it down.

    If I write it down, then it really happened.

    And I don't want it to have really happened.

    It's just some kind of a malfunction inside my head.

    A nightmare that I can wake up from.

    But if I don't write it down . . .

    Okay.

    I'll write it down.

    It happened so fast.

    I had no idea what was going on.

    Until I heard the scream.

    A girl started screaming as if her hair was on fire.

    And then the laughter started.

How dare he?!

My hands are shaking as I'm writing this.

Why did he do that?

VESPER

"Take the top card." Jonah looks at me. "Go on."

The four of us are sitting in a windy bit of the ship, but we have to. Jonah said it was really important that no one hears our conversation.

I look at Jonah's pack of cards, exactly the same kind that Amy had just now. What's he planning?

"We are not going to pick cards to decide who walks the plank," I say. "That's too gross for words. It's something that only someone like Jumper would come up with. I am not going to be a part of this."

"You'll have to if everyone else does" is all that Jonah says. "So are you going to pick a card or not? We're just practicing."

"No."

Then he holds out the cards to Gwen. "How about you?"

Jonah just shuffled the cards, and the two of hearts is

somewhere in there among the rest of the forty-eight cards. He jabbed a pen into it so Gwen can tell which card she's picking. The right one or the wrong one.

"Should I just pick one blind?" asks Gwen, but no one laughs. She takes the top card and runs her hand over it. "No dot. Which one is it?"

"King of diamonds," I say.

"That's right," says Jonah. "Now you two."

Reluctantly, I take a card.

"Six of hearts."

"Jack of clubs," says Bo.

"Great," says Jonah. "That's exactly how it should work."

"Okay . . ." I look at him. "But it could turn out differently, couldn't it? One of us could pick—"

"No," says Jonah. "That's not going to happen."

"How are you so certain of that?"

"Because the two of hearts"—without looking, Jonah swipes a few cards off the pile, and then the two of hearts falls onto the lounger—"is here."

"Huh?" Bo stares at him. "How did you know that?"

"Magic," Jonah says, blushing a little. "I'm a bit of a nerd, eh?"

Then I get it. "Y-you know card tricks." A flame flickers inside me. "So . . ."

"If I can get my hands on that pack of cards later, I can manipulate the results." Jonah rolls up the sleeves of his uniform. "Or at least I can make sure that *we* don't get that card. No promises about who *will* get it."

The wind suddenly seems to die down completely.

My brain is creaking like an old staircase.

"Do you realize that you're indirectly sending someone else onto the plank?" I ask quietly.

Jonah's red cheeks turn pale. "Yeah."

"And you're okay with that?"

"Of course not." Jonah's expression hardens. "But what are we supposed to do? Play fair? Do you want to walk out onto that diving board? Or do you want to watch while Gwen—"

"I'm going to puke." Gwen jumps up and I help her to the railing just in time. She throws up all her dinner. The sour smell makes me nauseous, but I keep stroking her back until she's done.

"Sorry," Gwen says, wiping her mouth.

"It's okay."

"All right." Jonah sweeps the cards back together. "So, do you guys trust me?"

"What if the trick goes wrong?" asks Bo.

"This trick never goes wrong," says Jonah. "Believe me, that two of hearts will end up with someone else."

* * *

Nine-thirty comes around way too quickly. It's freezing cold on the foredeck. I have goose bumps all over my body.

One of us is about to pick the wrong card. The chance is one in forty-nine.

At least, that's what everyone thinks. If I'm to believe Jonah, our chances are much better.

Is this okay?

We're making someone else walk the plank.

What if it's poor 20B? She survived the guards' attack, but her face is still black-and-blue.

Or maybe 17A will get it, the boy I've barely heard speak so far. I don't even know his name.

None of us deserves that card.

None of us should have to walk the plank.

Jonah's expression is tense, Gwen isn't saying a word, Bo is fiddling with the hem of her uniform.

"I could give some kind of speech, like Ted always does." Jumper looks around at the group. Even he seems nervous. "But I think we should just begin."

"Exactly." Amy takes out the pack of cards. "Here we go."

No one says much. It's as if everyone thinks talking might bring bad luck. As if you're doomed to pick the two of hearts as soon as you utter a single word.

"The person who picks the card has to walk the plank. All the way to the end. And stand there for one minute." Jumper looks at us. "If you refuse the challenge, we'll get the guards to lend a hand."

I think about Harrold.

"Who wants to shuffle?" Amy holds up the pack of cards.

"Give them here." Jonah takes the pack and removes the two of hearts. He pulls a pen from his pocket and presses the tip into the playing card.

"What are you doing?" yells Jumper.

"Chill." Jonah holds up the card, which now has a tiny dent in it. "This way, Gwen will know which card she has too."

Jonah slips the two of hearts back into the pack and shuffles the cards. It looks professional. "Pick one."

He holds out the cards to Amy.

"Why do I have to go first?" asks Amy.

"You don't. Who wants the first card?"

"Me." Bo takes a step forward. Her short blond hair is blowing in all directions. "Is that okay?"

She looks at Jonah. I know what she's really asking.

"Yep." Jonah holds out the cards to her. "Go ahead."

A terrible thought shoots through me: What if he's not actually to be trusted?

In documentaries, they sometimes talk about prisoners who are like that. They seem cool, but they're only looking out for themselves.

Who says that Jonah isn't just trying to save his own skin? Everyone here wants to survive. Everyone has to think about themselves.

Bo takes the top card from the stack. I want to yell at her to stop, but I don't do it.

Her hands are shaking so much that the card blows out of her hands and lands some distance away, with the face down.

"Which card is it?" someone shouts.

Bo walks over to it and bends down. When she turns it over, I can tell by her face that it's good news.

"Six of diamonds."

"Good," says Jonah. "Who's next?"

"I'll go now." Amy reaches out her hand. She's lucky, too.

"Gwen? Vesper?" Jonah holds out the pack. For a moment, I look into his latte macchiato eyes.

I remember how he lied to Gwen when she knocked over his glass of water. He said there was no damage done, but his sandwich was dripping wet.

Jonah cheered up Bo when she was so worried about Brian.

And he was honest about his victim and about hanging him up by his backpack.

Jonah might be a bully, but I can trust him.

"Want to do it together?" Gwen asks me.

I look at her. Her eyes are as frantic as when I first met her. Is she afraid that it's going to go wrong?

"You want to?"

"Yeah." Gwen takes the top card off the pack. The next one is mine.

My heart is racing so fast that I'm dizzy.

What if Jonah's trick doesn't work?

What if I have to walk the plank?

I could fall off. The wind is so strong.

An image of Ollie sitting with his front paws on my lap flashes into my head. He only ever does that when he's just been for a swim in the pond.

I hate it, but I'd give anything to smell that stink again.

"Want to turn them over?" I hear Gwen ask.

"Three, two, one..." I turn my card. When I see the red symbols my stomach clenches, but then I see what the card is. "Three of hearts!"

I shriek so loud that my voice cracks. "Three of hearts! Gwen!"

But then I see her standing there. Gwen is rubbing her thumb over the card, over and over again.

"What are you doing?" I take a step forward.

"Two of hearts." Gwen looks at me. Her eyes are filling with tears. "I've got the two of hearts."

1. ON BOARD

GWEN

The ship is enormous.

I might not be able to see it, but I can feel it. I can smell the saltwater, feel the sea breeze and the warmth of the sun, and I can hear the other passengers.

Mom and Dad cry as they hug me goodbye. I'm their only child, and I'm going on vacation on my own. It was Dad who brought the brochure home.

I think he's still getting used to the fact that I can't see anymore, because he handed it to me as if I'd be able to do something with it.

As always, Mom described to me in detail what was in the brochure.

A vacation like this would make me more resilient, she said. I understand why they think that's necessary.

According to my new mentor, I have a very anxious look in my eyes. I have no idea what she means. I just think my eyes are hanging around uselessly in their sockets. At least, that's what I remember blind people's eyes looking like.

"Good luck, sweetheart." Mom gives me another hug, as if she's regretting the plan to let me go.

"Gwen Molenburg?" A woman with a supersweet voice welcomes me on board. "Will you come with me? There's someone who'd like to speak to you before we set off."

I almost trip over the end of the gangway, but then I'm safe on board.

"Who?"

"Ted. He's the organizer of this trip."

Trip.

I remember the brochure. The way Mom described it, it sounded so . . . real.

Could I be wrong?

Am I *really* going sailing on a ship for ten days and enjoying a vacation?

"I'm Tina, by the way, one of the supervisors. If there are any problems, you can always talk to me."

A door opens. I hear a man's voice telling us to come in.

"I'm Ted," he says. His voice is very different than Tina's. Low and kind of trembly. "Why don't you sit down, Gwen?"

"Thank you." I find a soft seat behind me and lower myself onto it.

"Welcome to the ship, Gwen. I wanted to talk to you before the trip begins."

"Do you do that with everyone?"

I hear a chuckle.

"No, Gwen. I don't do that with everyone."

That's nothing new, the way he keeps saying my name. Since I've been blind, people do it all the time. Like I'm not going to realize they're talking to me otherwise.

"So why me?"

"Because of your visual . . . impairment."

I hate that word.

"It's possible that the next few days will be difficult for you because you can't see," says Tina.

"Why would this *vacation* be difficult for me?" I put extra emphasis on the word *vacation* and calmly wait for them to respond.

The silence lasts a little too long. That tells me all I need to know.

"This is the No Exit program, isn't it?"

There's such an extreme silence that I think for a moment that they've left the room. But then I hear Ted cough.

"What do you know about No Exit, Gwen?"

"I've heard the rumors."

"And what do you think about it?"

"It's a great idea." I weigh my words carefully. "Bullying should be punished."

"Have you been bullied?"

"Sure."

"And you've bullied other people?"

I hear the screaming again.

All this time I thought I had to be a bully in order to come here. I didn't have a choice.

But I also felt something else. Something I'm still ashamed of.

I felt so powerful.

"Yes."

"Why did you start bullying if you'd heard the rumors?" Ted asks. "You didn't actually want to end up here, did you?"

"Sure did."

I could bite my tongue. Why am I telling him this?

"You *wanted* to come here?" Ted asks in surprise.

I can't back out now. I have to say it.

"Yes, I wanted to come."

"But why?"

"Because of Jumper." Saying his name out loud is harder than I thought.

Complete silence. The ship slowly sways back and forth.

For the first time, I wonder if I made the right decision. What if the whole plan goes wrong? Maybe he won't even be here.

"Jumper, you say?" Ted sounds puzzled.

"Yeah. That's obviously not his real name, but it's what

he calls himself." I remember the post that Jumper put on social media a while ago. "He killed someone."

"Killed someone?" Ted echoes.

I think of Rixt.

"Yes. My best friend. Last winter."

More silence.

Why aren't they saying anything?

"Okay. Gwen"—Ted clears his throat—"what were you planning to do to Jumper?"

I look up. At times like this, I hate that I can't see anything. I want to look this man in the face, to see how he's looking at me.

But I have to make do with my intuition. I have to take the chance that they won't just hand me over to the police.

"I want to . . . He needs to die," I say quietly. "For what he did."

Yet more silence.

They must think I'm crazy.

But then Ted snaps his fingers. "Tina, you go look after the others. Welcome them and escort them to their cabins for my video message. No exceptions. I'll take care of . . . *this*."

"Will do." I hear the door open and close, and then I'm alone with Ted.

"Gwen," he says slowly. "I'm going to be very honest with you. Is that okay?"

It seems to have become a few degrees cooler in the room. I don't like this man. I'm sure of that now. "Yes."

"No Exit is against violence, but sometimes I believe that violence is the only solution. Your plan sounds impossible, but maybe it *is* possible because"—I feel his eyes running over me—"because no one would suspect you."

I nod. I know exactly what he means. The poor, pathetic, little blind girl.

"And it's important that it stay that way."

"What do you mean?"

"You'll have to find some way not to attract attention."

"I've already thought about that," I say, putting on a sappy little voice. "I'm *innocent*. I don't belong here."

"Exactly." I hear something in Ted's voice that sounds like admiration. "Something like that. You'll have to react as if you're stunned when you hear my video message. If anyone realizes that you actually wanted to end up here..."

"I can do that," I say. "We have drama lessons at school. I've learned that you need to stay close to the real you when you're playing a role. So I did know about No Exit, but only as a rumor."

"Good. And Jumper... How are you planning to...?"

I can hardly believe we're discussing this.

"I'm not sure yet."

"But he doesn't recognize you?"

"No."

"Perfect." Ted's chair squeaks. "Tina and I will treat you like all the other bullies from now on. You'll be on your own. We'll give you complete freedom to carry out your plan, Gwen, but don't expect any cooperation."

I nod. My intuition was right. They won't hand me over to the police. They're going to let me be free to do what I want.

"And the most important thing: Everything that was said here will remain within these four walls. This conversation never happened."

GWEN

"You okay?" Jonah asks when Vesper doesn't react.

"That's not possible," she says.

"Of course it is. Anything is possible here."

"But surely not without any consequences? I mean, the government . . . and my dad. He'd never have signed me up for this if he thought that . . ."

"They'll obviously tell them a different story. If someone dies, it'll be a 'tragic accident.' Anyway, there's too much evidence that the program works. Anyone who makes it through No Exit will think twice before they bully someone again."

"But what about the ship?" asks Vesper. "Who's paying for all this?"

"Ted." I can tell from his voice that Jonah is leaning forward. "The captain, the guy on TV. He's apparently a billionaire."

I have to say something now. If I stay too quiet, they'll notice.

"It's pretty smart," I say. "A ship like this. There's nowhere to go. We're miles from anywhere."

"So that others will be safe." Jonah imitates the voice from the video perfectly. "Everyone wants to get rid of us. School, parents, the government... They'll do whatever it takes to change us. But first they have to break us."

"What do you mean?"

"That's the order they do it in. Break you, reshape you, and hand you back. With some people, that takes a lot of work."

I think about my mom and dad.

What were they thinking when they signed me up for this project? Were they ashamed that I'm their daughter?

Blind.

And a bully too.

"Some people are rotten through and through," I hear Jonah say. Who's he talking about?

Does he mean Jumper?

In that case, I like Jonah even more.

"And if that doesn't work, they just *kill* you?" Vesper sounds like she doesn't believe a word of it.

"Exactly. If we don't make enough of an improvement, they throw us overboard. 'Oops, it was an accident! She was standing too close to the edge and there was a big wave, your honor.'"

"Don't be so weird."

"I believe it," I say quietly. "No one's going to miss a bully."

"You said you were innocent, didn't you?" Vesper asks me.

"Of course she's innocent," says Jonah.

"Why do you say that?"

"Because she..." I can feel Jonah sizing me up. I know what he's thinking. It's all going exactly as Ted predicted: people don't think I really count. Like I'm not taking part in life anymore. At least, not really.

"Because she's way too nice."

That wasn't what he wanted to say, but it's nice of him to try to spare my feelings.

"I *am* innocent," I say. I have to convince them or this isn't going to work. "But on board this ship, I'm as much of a bully as the rest of you. There's no way they're going to let me off."

GWEN

"Good evening, Bullies." Ted's voice booms around our cabin. I feel my whole body freeze. "The first night is always the hardest, but hey, you're off to a good start."

A good start.

How can he say something like that after today?

Someone is dead.

Dead.

I didn't see anything, but I felt the death in every cell in my body.

"We have a tough schedule programmed for tomorrow, so make sure to get a good rest. You're going to need all your energy."

The screen goes off. I hear Vesper's restless breathing. Is she thinking about 4B now too? Or about the cabin across the corridor? I can tell that there's something going on between Jonah and Vesper. I'm not stupid. She likes him, or he likes her, or they both like each other.

"Do you think Jumper will keep his fists to himself tonight?" I ask.

"No," she says immediately. I can hear the fear in Vesper's voice.

"Can I ask you something?" I say. "Why do you hate it so much when people cry? Does it have to do with your mom?"

She doesn't reply.

"Vesper?" She's pretending to be asleep, but I'm not falling for that. I know exactly how to get her talking.

"I'm sorry." I say, sobbing quietly. "I shouldn't have asked. I—I do get it. I—" More sobbing.

"Oh, just shut your mouth," Vesper growls.

I chuckle. "Then tell me why."

"Crying makes no sense."

"Why not?"

"It doesn't bring anyone back. Everyone cried at Mom's funeral. No one could make it to the end of their speeches. It was so awkward."

"You think?"

"Yeah. Dad was blubbing away like some little eight-year-old kid."

"And you didn't cry?"

"No, never."

"Could that be why you're so mad? Because you couldn't cry?"

"What do you mean?"

"Because you feel guilty? You know, about your mom. Because it feels like you're not sad about her death?"

"That's bullshit."

But I know that it's not bullshit.

When Rixt died, I couldn't cry either. It was like my body refused to cooperate. Just like the day I went blind.

The black spots appeared out of nowhere. I thought at first it was because of the heat. I'd had blackouts before, but this time it didn't stop. When Dad came into the room, all I could see was a shadow. His face was just a black blob.

I pull the covers up over me. Going up and down on the waves is making me feel nauseous.

Why couldn't I cry about Rixt? Didn't she mean enough to me? Or was it because she meant too much?

Maybe I'd go on crying forever once I started.

Maybe I'd drown, too.

"Gwen?"

I can't bring myself to reply. Instead, I squeeze my eyes shut and pretend to be asleep.

GWEN

"Take the top card," Jonah urges. "Go on."

"We are not going to pick cards to decide who walks the plank," says Vesper. "That's too gross for words. It's something that only someone like Jumper would come up with. I am not going to be a part of this."

I feel sick.

Because I know what's going to happen. Because I know I have to do this.

Because Rixt was my best friend.

The wind is blowing my hair all over the place.

"How about you?" I can hear that Jonah is holding out the pack of cards to me. I know he made a tiny dent in the two of hearts. We have braille playing cards at school that we use to play all kinds of games.

"Should I just pick one blind?" I laugh nervously. What if they realize what I'm up to?

My hands shaking, I take the top playing card and run my thumb over it. There's no dent.

"No dot. Which one is it?"

"King of diamonds," says Vesper.

Then Vesper picks the six of hearts, and Bo the jack of clubs.

"Great," says Jonah. "That's exactly how it should work."

"Okay . . . ," says Vesper. "But it could turn out differently, couldn't it? One of us could pick—"

"No," says Jonah. "That's not going to happen."

"How are you so certain of that?"

"Because the two of hearts"—I hear a card fall to the ground—"is here."

"Huh?" Bo gasps. "How did you know that?"

"Magic," says Jonah. "I'm a bit of a nerd, eh?"

"Y-you know card tricks," Vesper stammers. "So . . ."

"If I can get my hands on that pack of cards later, I can manipulate the results. Or at least I can make sure that *we* don't get that card. No promises about who *will* get it."

"Do you realize that you're indirectly sending someone else onto the plank?" Vesper says quietly.

Jonah's voice sounds small when he says, "Yeah."

"And you're okay with that?"

I can hear something in her voice. Is she disappointed in him?

"Of course not," says Jonah. "But what are we supposed

to do? Play fair? Do you want to walk out onto that diving board? Or do you want to watch while Gwen—"

"I'm going to puke." I jump to my feet. Reach the railing just in time. I feel Vesper's hand on my back, but that just makes it worse. I can't stop throwing up.

I can't do this.

I mustn't do this.

She'll feel guilty forever.

And what about Jonah?

He'll think his trick didn't work.

Jumper had one victim.

But how many am I about to have?

Vesper and Jonah are my friends. Crazily, they're more my friends than I should ever have allowed.

I began this journey alone, and I should have stayed alone.

"Sorry," I say when I've finally stopped vomiting.

"It's okay." Vesper has no idea why I said sorry, and I can't tell her anything.

"All right. So, do you guys trust me?" asks Jonah.

I think about the two of hearts. All I have to do is bring an extra two of hearts with me. The plan is watertight. So why does it feel as if I'm going to throw up again?

"What if the trick goes wrong?" asks Bo.

"This trick never goes wrong," says Jonah. "Believe me, that two of hearts will end up with someone else."

5. OVERBOARD

VESPER

"Two of hearts." Gwen looks at me. Her eyes are filling with tears. "I've got the two of hearts."

"What?" My voice catches in my throat. "How . . . ?"

Gwen holds up her card. When I see the two red hearts, my stomach does a backflip.

"Ha!" Jumper's voice flashes like lightning. "Then you're walking the plank!"

When I look up, I see the shock on the others' faces. But at the same time, I see something else.

Relief.

Because they don't have to do it.

"No," I say. "No, she's not walking the plank."

"She has to." Jumper takes a step forward. "That was the deal."

"Screw the deal!" I stand between him and Gwen.

"And what if I'd picked the card?" asks Jumper. "Would you have made such a scene?"

I bite the inside of my cheek until it bleeds. How did this happen? How did Gwen get the two of hearts? Jonah said it was impossible!

"Are you coming?" Jumper asks Gwen.

"Just shut up!" I scream. That plank is way too dangerous. The wind will blow her straight into the water. "Gwen's not going anywhere!"

"What's going on?" Tina's voice startles us. "What's all this shouting about?"

"She"—Jumper points at Gwen—"picked the card, so now she has to walk the plank."

"We're playing a game," says Amy. "The loser has to walk to the end of the plank and stand there for a minute."

"But if she wants to, she's free to jump," Jumper begins, but Tina interrupts him.

"Twenty-Five B?" Tina looks at Gwen. "Is this true?"

Gwen turns her card in her hand. I just want to snatch it from her and tear it into a thousand pieces.

"I did lose," Gwen says quietly.

"No," I say again. "You don't need to walk that plank. I'll . . ."

"Yeah, I do." Gwen looks up. I feel like she's looking straight at me. Her eyes, normally so frantic, are completely focused. "I have to walk the plank."

"Want me to help you?" I hear Jumper ask.

"Keep your hands off her!" I go to stop him, but then Gwen wraps her arms around me. Tight, as if I'm her life buoy. She puts her lips to my ear and whispers three words: "Let me go."

I know there's no way she can know about Mom.

That those were her last three words.

All the strength drains from my body.

Gwen kisses the spot right next to my ear. And then she lets go of me.

"If you want to help, you're welcome," I hear her say to Jumper.

What's she doing? Why would she let *him* help her?

Dazed, I just stare at the scene unfolding in front of me.

"Need a hand to get up there?" I hear Jumper ask.

"Please." Gwen steps onto the plank. In the darkness, I can just make out her silhouette, her hair fluttering around her face.

"Gwen!" I finally come to my senses. She has to get off that plank. The wind is way too strong.

But Gwen slowly shuffles forward. And then, a couple of steps from the end, she stops.

"Stand there for one minute," shouts Jumper. "The countdown begins . . . now."

It suddenly becomes very quiet on deck. The only

sound is coming from the wind and from my own heartbeat, thumping loudly in my ears.

Why is this happening?

Why did she get the two of hearts?

Why am I letting this happen?

She's blind. This is way too dangerous!

And why did she tell me to let her go? I should have done it myself!

"Almost there," shouts Jumper. "Ten, nine . . ."

"Can you help me back?" asks Gwen.

"Go on, then." Jumper holds out his hand. "Take my hand. Six, five . . ."

Gwen gropes around.

"I'm here. Four, three . . ." Jumper looks at his watch again.

And that's when it happens.

She grabs his arm, just like she did with me all those times.

"Ow." Jumper looks at her. "What are you doing?"

"We're going to jump, Jumper."

"What?!" Jumper looks in panic at her hand on his wrist. He tries to pull away, but almost stumbles dangerously. "Let go of me!"

"This is for Rixt," I hear Gwen say.

"Rixt?" Jumper yells. "Who the—"

"Her name was Rixt, not Romeo," Gwen yells above the sound of the roaring waves. "And she was a girl."

And then she leaps, pulling Jumper with her in her fall.

"Gwen!" My voice is lost in the wind.

I run to the railing. Beneath me, there is nothing but churning seawater.

"I can't see her."

"Of course not!" someone shouts. "The sea's way too rough."

"Where are they?" Amy comes to stand beside me. "Jumper!"

"Remove her," I hear Tina say.

Two guards take Amy away. She's screaming all kinds of things, but her words are lost on me.

Gwen.

Gwen's in the sea.

Why is no one doing anything?

But the ship sails on.

Gwen must be far behind us by now.

Maybe deep underwater.

I remember the moment when I was thrown overboard. The sea doesn't play fair.

She's not going to survive.

"Gwen! Gwen! Gwen!" I keep shouting her name as if I'm throwing a rope with a life buoy attached.

I have to go after her, to look for her.

She's blind. She can't win this . . .

I place my foot on the bottom bar of the railing, but then I feel two hands on my upper arms.

"Vesper." It's Jonah, pulling me back.

I turn to look at him. "You . . . You said it would work!"

I pound my fists on his chest.

And I keep on hitting.

Like it makes some kind of difference.

"It would have worked . . ." Jonah just lets me go on thumping him. "It would have worked if . . ."

Then he holds up two cards with two hearts on them. "If there hadn't been two of these cards."

"What . . ." I stare at the two identical cards. Each has a tiny dent in the middle. The braille card.

"There were two of them, Vesper." Jonah's voice cracks. "Gwen wanted to practice the trick. I gave her a pack of cards. She had an extra two of hearts."

"What . . ." I can't even speak. I feel as if I'm a two of hearts myself. As if my heart is breaking in two.

"Gwen must have wanted this to happen." Jonah's eyes are darting in all directions, just like Gwen's. "And I have no idea why."

* * *

The empty mattress on the floor by my bed seems to be grinning up at me.

Gwen's duvet is heaped at the foot of the bed.

For a second, it feels as if she's hiding there.

As if she could come out from under it at any moment and shout, "Here I am! I'm back!"

But Jonah's hand on my shoulder tells me that she won't. He gently pushes me into the room.

"You have ten minutes," the guard tells me. "Then you have to go back to the others."

I'm too exhausted to object.

"What are we looking for?" asks Jonah when we're on our own.

"Something," I say. "Anything. A goodbye letter, a final message, whatever it might be."

Jonah pulls the duvet off the mattress. Then he goes into Gwen's section of the cabin. I hear him rummaging around in the closet.

What if she didn't leave anything behind? What if I never find out why she . . . My throat feels tight and sore.

No trace of any note or anything else.

Her name was Rixt, not Romeo. And she was a girl.

Gwen's last words echo inside my head.

Rixt.

Romeo.

I don't get it.

What does Gwen's best friend have to do with Jumper's victim?

"You found anything?" Jonah shouts from Gwen's room.

"No." I look around. There aren't that many hiding places here.

Maybe I need to accept that there isn't anything. That she just jumped.

But why?

Because.

"I can't do this," I whisper. "I need a reason." I drop onto my bed.

And then I feel it: something hard under my butt.

I jump up and slide my hand under the duvet. My fingers find the hard cover of a book.

When I pull it out, I see the letters. Some of the words have been scribbled out, but the scribbles have been partially erased. The writing is messy, but legible.

"Jonah . . ." My voice catches in my throat.

This is a thousand times better than a note.

This is a diary.

We take it to the top deck. And there, beneath the stars, we start reading.

DIARY OF RIXT & GWEN

He suddenly came and sat across from me at breaktime today. Started eating his sandwich, calm as anything, like it was completely normal for him to be sitting there.

As he chewed, he kept staring at me, like I was an animal in the zoo.

Chew.
Gulp.
Stare.
Chew.
Gulp.
Stare.
Made me really nervous.
Could he see that I'd padded my bra?
He can't know about that. Can he?
When he'd finally finished his sandwich, he just smiled.
He stood up and walked away.

Reading this makes me so mad.
  You don't deserve this!
  Sadly, I know how you feel.
  People stare at me all day long.
  Like they think a blind person doesn't realize.
  I wish they'd make it illegal to stare at people.

"This diary belongs to Rixt and Gwen," Jonah says, his eyes widening.

I stare at the bottom few lines, which are a lot harder to read than the top ones. Two sets of handwriting. Two friends.

"Rixt was the one who was mur—" Jonah begins, but I'm reading again.

Reading some of the pages in their entirety, skimming others, searching for clues.

Today he said no one will ever dare to kiss me.
  That I'm a freak.
  That it's a shame I was ever born.
  That I'll never be a real girl.

But you are a girl!

If I could, I'd lock him up.

Far away from the outside world.

That might be even better than killing him. Then I'd have all the time and space I needed to do whatever I wanted to him.

"No . . ." The situation is slowly dawning on me. "Rixt was transgender."

There are days when I want to kill him. And days when I want to kill myself.

I would love to escape from this body.

But I'm stuck in it.

—

Ultimately, I don't think I could ever do that.

Suicide, I mean.

You couldn't either, could you?

I feel sick, but I still keep on reading.

I'm so scared that he knows, Gwen.

—

I feel so powerless.

I just wish I could go to your school, instead of that dumb school for blind kids.

Then we could help each other.

—

Right in the middle of the schoolyard, he put his hand on my chest.

His gross, disgusting hand gave it a squeeze.

And as he did it, he looked at me.

I knew right away that he could feel the padding.

Now he knows.

Oh no, he knows.

My tears are making my words blur.

Can you still feel the letters?

I'm trying to press into the paper as hard as I can.

—

DON'T CRY.

Dear Rixt, he doesn't deserve your tears.

He doesn't deserve a single tear from you.

And yes, I can still understand everything perfectly.

* * *

It's like I'm watching a movie that I already know the ending of. You want to yell at the lead actor: Don't do it, don't go into that cellar! Don't marry that man! Don't believe that cop!

I have the same feeling now.

Because I know this is not going to end well.

He called me a dick today.

In front of everyone.

Just to see how I'd react.

I just walked on by, but I could feel my cheeks burning. I hoped that would be the end of it, but I heard a few people laughing.

And laughter is like fuel for him.

It's what keeps him going.

He yelled after me: "Romeo, oh, Romeo! Wherefore art thou Romeo?"

It felt like I was breaking into a thousand pieces.

He knows my old name.

"Romeo?" The color drains from Jonah's face. "But that's . . ."

"I know." My eyes are flying along the lines.

My hands are shaking as I'm writing this.

How dare he call you Romeo?

You're Rixt.

You're the most beautiful girl I've ever seen. Yeah, I know what you're going to say: I can't actually see you.

But I know it's true.

You've always been a girl.

He needs to be stopped.

For good.

—

Did I ever tell you I used to be jealous of you? Whenever we braided each other's hair, I deliberately took a long time.

Your hair was so soft.

I had long hair too at the time, of course, but it felt different.

Rougher.

Like long boy's hair.

I wanted girl's hair.

Maybe I'll never become a real girl.

The thought of him telling *everyone* that I'm a boy.

That can't happen.

That mustn't happen.

—

Hang in there.
    Not much longer and you'll be out of that place.
    You're getting hormones, and you'll finally be who you've always been.
    And you have beautiful hair.

—

Please tell me something hopeful.
    Tell me the world's not as rotten as it seems.

—

Think about fun things.
    Think about extra-big scoops of ice cream.
    Or a short line at the roller coaster.
    Think about the summer and coming with us to Italy. We'll buy the most stunning bikini to celebrate that you're done at that dumbass school.
    And the most amazing Italian guy will flirt with you.
    He'll tell you you're the most beautiful girl in the world.
    Ciao bella!

—

Today on the school trip he finally did what I've been afraid of all this time.

I can't even write it down.

If I write it down, then it really happened.

And I don't want it to have really happened.

It's just some kind of a malfunction inside my head.

A nightmare that I can wake up from.

But if I don't write it down...

Okay.

I'll write it down.

He pulled down my pants.

It happened so fast.

I had no idea what was going on.

Until I heard the scream.

A girl started screaming as if her hair was on fire.

And then the laughter started.

It's like I'm there. I can see it happening: Rixt frantically trying to pull her pants back up, even though everyone has already seen.

The part of herself that she desperately tries to keep hidden because it's not really a part of her.

How dare he?!

My hands are shaking as I'm writing this.

Why did he do that?

What did you ever do to him?

* * *

"It was Jumper," says Jonah breathlessly. "Jumper was the one who destroyed Rixt."

"Jumper murdered Rixt," I say. "That was how Gwen saw it."

That sentence echoes through my head:

What did you ever do to him?
What did you ever do to him?
What did you ever do to him?
What did you ever do to him?
What did you ever do to him?
What did you ever do to him?
Nothing.

Rixt was a girl, but Jumper couldn't handle that. He was determined to break her. By calling her "Romeo," by squeezing her breasts, and by exposing her in front of the whole school.

"Rixt wrote something else," says Jonah.

This is our story, Gwen.
 I've made everything I crossed out readable again.
 Who cares if someone finds this diary?
 No one cares how we feel.
 He's just going to keep on going around at school, doing the same thing and making my life hell.

I can't do this anymore.

I'm sorry.

How must have Gwen felt when she read that? Did she get a ride over to Rixt's house?

And was that when she found out she was too late?

That Rixt had already taken her own life?

She jumped off a bridge and into the water.

All because Jumper wanted to break her. And he succeeded.

I try to put myself in Gwen's shoes, but I can't do it. Cancer took Mom from me, but cancer isn't a person. I can get mad at a few tumors, but that isn't a flesh-and-blood human being.

Not a person who's happily getting on with his life and actually calling himself Jumper.

As if he's proud of what he did.

And then on the last few pages, I see Gwen's handwriting again. It's even harder to read than before, as if she had to write this bit in a hurry.

It's real!

No Exit exists—and I'm in.

* * *

"Huh?" says Jonah, reading over my shoulder. "This sounds almost like she was happy to be on board."

They've destroyed everything!
    All because of 9A.
    But this diary is still here.
    I'm an expert at hiding stuff!
    I need to make sure no one finds this diary.
    At least, not until the end.
    I don't know exactly when that will be, but my plan can't fail.
    Ted and Tina have promised that I'm free to do what I want.

Ted and Tina?
    So, she wrote this part on board! And I had no idea.
    Did she do it under the covers?
    I look up, but we're still alone. They're going to come for us soon, but luckily not yet.

Can I go through with this plan?
    Vesper and Jonah are so nice.
    For the first time, I feel like I've got a group of friends.
    Like it doesn't matter to them that I can't see.
    I don't know if I can betray them . . .

* * *

I don't want to go on reading, but it's as if the words are pulling me along.

No...

They've all been injured because of me.

Ted and Tina told everyone that the attack in the dark was 4B's karma, but of course it wasn't.

It was *my* karma.

There's only one person here who has the advantage in the dark.

When I was back for a day at my old high school, a former "friend" went to the bathroom.

One of the friends who abandoned me by the slides.

One flick of the switch—and the bathrooms were in darkness.

I heard her scream.

I attacked her, hit her as hard as I could with my cane.

While I shouted the most horrible things at her. So, she knew it was me, but that was the idea.

I had to get to No Exit.

Because if the program really existed, Jumper would be there.

Rixt's mom and dad told me he'd been enrolled in a

reeducation program. Where I'd have ten days to get revenge for Rixt.

"S-so she got locked up here on purpose?" Jonah stammers.

But I wasn't sent to No Exit.
  People got it.
  They understood why I'd attacked that girl.
  Everyone always feels so sorry for blind people.
  So, I had to go a step further. I had to become a *real* bully.
  I didn't want to do it.
  But I had to.
  For Rixt.
  How else was I going to get so close to Jumper?

"So that's why," begins Jonah, "that's why she said we didn't have to bully people for someone else. I remember thinking it was an odd choice of words."

I've spotted my chance.
  Jumper came up with the idea himself: whoever picks the two of hearts has to walk the plank.

Jonah's going to make sure that we don't pick that card.
But what if I do pick it and I can overpower Jumper?
There's no other way I can murder him.
He's way stronger than I am.
I know exactly what I need to do.
No one will see it coming.
Who's the blind one here? ☺

"We were," I say quietly. "We were the blind ones."

"You had no way of knowing," says Jonah. "Seriously."

I look at Gwen's last line.

The smiley at the end is a bit smudged. I'm sure it's because she was crying. When I couldn't see her, of course.

She wrote it all down in that almost illegible scribble. Because she was in a hurry and because she couldn't see what she was writing.

But she still made the effort. For herself or for me?

It doesn't matter.

Now I understand why.

6. LAND IN SIGHT

VESPER

"Twenty-Five A." Tina comes onto the rear deck. "There you are."

Just the sound of her voice makes me cringe. Why won't she just leave me alone?

Since Gwen died, she seems to be watching me constantly. She's nearby during every new karmic assignment.

Tina's around when I eat, when I sit by the pool with Jonah, when I talk to Bo.

Jonah says she's afraid of what I know.

That maybe Gwen told me too much.

And she did.

We even have it in writing. I'm sure that Gwen did that on purpose.

Ted and Tina have promised that I'm free to do what I want.

As soon as we get home, I'm taking her diary to the media. Someone has to make sure that No Exit is shut down.

I clutch the diary even more tightly to me. I keep it in the inside pocket of my uniform, close to my heart.

"What do you want?" Jonah stands in front of me like a bodyguard.

"Twenty-Five A, come with me. Ted wants to speak to you."

Ted? The last time he wanted to speak to me, he tried to convince me that he was right, and he showed me the urn. So close and yet out of my reach.

"No, thank you," I say.

Tina is still smiling. "It wasn't a question."

Tina walks ahead of me. We come to a door with a sign on it: ACCESS FORBIDDEN BEYOND THIS POINT.

We head straight through the door.

This is the section where our victims are staying! I look around—the corridors appear to be just the same as in our part of the ship. Cabin doors on both sides.

When we're all the way on the other side of the ship, Tina finally comes to a stop.

"You can wait here." She sends me into a room. "Ted will be here soon."

I sit down on the wooden chair in front of the desk. The room seems familiar, as if I've been here before.

Mom's urn!

I jump to my feet. Up on the top shelf of the cabinet behind the desk, I see Mom.

Just sitting there, as if she's been waiting patiently for me all this time.

As quickly as I can, I push Ted's desk chair over to the cabinet and climb up onto it. I grab the urn off the shelf and hug it to my chest.

"Twenty-Five A." Ted's voice booms into the room.

I spin around, almost falling off the chair. Where's the screen?

But then I realize. Ted isn't on a screen.

He's here for real.

He's standing in the doorway, looking at me, fingers resting on the door handle.

I climb down from the chair, still clutching the urn. If he thinks he's going to take it from me again, I'll fight for it. I'll fight as if my whole life depends on it.

"I see you've found the urn." Ted closes the door behind him.

I just nod. I can't seem to speak.

"Sit down." Ted points at the wooden chair. Then he brushes the imaginary dirt from his chair and drops down onto it.

"You surprise me," he says then. "You're still just as rebellious as you were ten days ago."

"That doesn't surprise me" is all I say.

Ted leans back in his chair. "The project ends today. How do you look back on these ten days?"

I gaze outside. The endless sea. Gwen's final resting place.

Gwen.

Don't think about her.

It hurts so much that it feels as if I'm falling apart into millions of pieces.

"Twenty-Five A?"

I don't reply. I'm not in the mood for questions, and certainly not that kind of question.

No Exit is not a good system. It's a place that's only about death and destruction.

"I'm so curious about what goes on inside your heads." Ted tilts his head. "It would help us so much in our . . ."

As if we're a bunch of lab rats.

And maybe that's how Ted sees us. How else could anyone keep running a project like this? Year after year?

"Do you really want to know?" I ask.

Ted nods. "Sure do."

I'm going to go to the police. The whole world will find out how sick No Exit is. I'm going to get revenge for Gwen. Here's her diary. Go ahead and read it. You're in it, you disgusting, deranged . . .

But then it's as if I hear Gwen's voice in my ear:
Simmer down. I need you.

All that time, she was right. There's no point fighting, not here on board. That won't get you anywhere.

But once we're on dry land, Ted won't be in charge anymore. When we're ashore, I'll get him. And Tina. And Harrold. And all those other guards.

"You were right," I say.

Ted looks at me.

"No Exit works." Now I have to keep going. "I was wrong."

"Really?" Ted says with a frown. He doesn't believe me.

"I'll never bully anyone again," I say. "Truly. Never again."

That's not a lie. Whenever anyone mentions bullying, I'll remember the last ten days. But that doesn't mean No Exit works, does it?

"That's good to hear," says Ted. "If we get through to just one person, it was all worth it."

I look back outside. Will I ever be able to see the sea without thinking about Gwen?

For the first two days, I was convinced she was going to

turn up. That she'd suddenly appear at breakfast or lying on the mattress beside my bed.

But I've spent the past few days staring out at the sea to see if I could spot her body anywhere.

I know neither is going to happen. She's not coming back, and she won't have a funeral. At least, there won't be anything inside the casket.

Her death is invisible.

But I will never forget her.

"You can go, Vesper."

I clutch the urn more tightly as I stand up. Ted doesn't demand to have it back. He actually lets me leave.

As I close the door behind me and head back to my cabin, it dawns on me. Ted just called me by my real name.

"The urn." Jonah looks at me in amazement. "You got it back!"

I nod and zip up my duct-taped backpack, then sling the straps over my shoulders.

"I'm not taking this off until we get home."

Home.

I picture Dad. Will he be waiting on the quayside when we get there?

Does he want me back?

And what do I want?

He signed that agreement. Did he know what he was getting me into?

What will he say when I tell him about everything that happened here?

About karma, the isolation cell, 4B, Gwen . . .

"If you don't want to live at home anymore, then you can come to my place." Jonah is standing beside me. We're staring ahead—not at the sea, but above it. I think we've both had enough of the ocean for a lifetime.

"Or mine," says a voice behind us.

We turn around. Brian and Bo are standing behind us on the deck, holding hands. Brian's face is still badly swollen, but his eyes are bright.

"Brian!" Jonah shouts with a grin. "You're back!"

"More or less." Brian holds out his hand to Jonah. "Thanks for everything."

"What for?" Jonah asks, surprised.

"You kept my favorite number alive." He glances at Bo. "Thanks to your card trick . . ."

But then his face clouds over. "I'm so sorry about Gwen."

I feel a lump in my throat, and I swallow hard.

It doesn't work. The lump is still there.

"I mean it. Both of you can come live with me. I'm sure my mom won't mind." Brian raises his hand. "Okay. See you later."

They walk on, hand in hand. Jonah and I watch them go.

"I don't think his mom would be too happy to have three extra bullies around the place," says Jonah. "How about you?"

I smile. The lump gets just a little bit smaller. "Yeah, me neither."

Jonah leans back and lets fly.

A big blob of spit whizzes through the air.

"Charming," I say.

Jonah nudges me. "Your turn."

I do the same. The spit covers much more distance than it did on the first day.

"You've been practicing," says Jonah.

"No, not really."

Jonah looks to one side, and I follow his gaze. Brian and Bo are on the other side of the deck, kissing. They seem to have forgotten that we're still here.

"Maybe we should do that too," I hear Jonah say.

"What?"

"Kiss," says Jonah. "Do you want to?"

"You're crazy," I say, but I can feel something in my stomach that has nothing to do with the rocking of the waves.

Jonah grins. "Yeah, maybe a bit, eh?"

Then his expression suddenly becomes serious. "It's not your fault, okay? Gwen wanted it herself."

"I know." I've reread her diary a hundred times, but it doesn't really help.

Why didn't she say anything to me? I could have helped her. We could have pushed Jumper overboard together, the two of us, then she wouldn't have had to jump with him.

"Promise me you won't keep on feeling guilty." Jonah looks at me sternly. "Promise me."

"What about you?" I look at him. He hasn't touched a playing card since. And when Brian just mentioned his trick, I saw the look of pain on his face.

"I'll try." Jonah pushes himself off the railing. "I'm going to get something to eat before we arrive. I'll bring something for you."

When Jonah's gone, I take out the diary. Yet again, I open it and start reading, soaking up Gwen's final sentences like a sponge.

Jonah's right. It's what she wanted.

I have to keep reminding myself of that.

But then my eye falls on the last page. It seems to have been taped to the back cover.

Why didn't I notice that before?

With my nail, I unpick the tape—and I feel my heart leap.

There are a few more sentences written on the inside of the cover. Gwen's very last words of all.

I didn't cry after Rixt died either.
>Some things are too big to cry about.
>But you can cry now, dear Vesper.
>It's allowed.

And finally, I let my tears go.

MAREN STOFFELS
ABOUT *DEEP WATER*

This story was in my head for more than six years. Every year I thought: Now I have to write it. But that didn't happen. Other stories had priority, and this felt like a huge project, as huge as No Exit itself.

Could I actually write this book?

A bunch of bullies on a ship—and some of them die, too?

Would people want to read that?

Could I make it believable?

For this book, I interviewed three people, each with their own extraordinary story.

Joseph was imprisoned for a few years in Morocco even though he was innocent, and his bizarre life story formed the basis of this book. Even though conditions in prisons vary throughout the world, none are hotels. Because you can check out of a hotel. You're in prison 24/7.

Just like on this luxury cruise ship . . .

Noa told me about going blind. Five years ago, almost overnight, she started to see spots. And then suddenly she couldn't see her dad anymore.

When I visited her school, I gained a lot of inspiration for Gwen.

And then there was the story of Maria, who was seriously bullied as a child. That kind of thing leaves scars, sometimes for a whole lifetime. You really don't want to think about some of the terrible things that people can do to each other. . . .

It felt as if I was ready: The book could be written. And the words came streaming out of me.

The story felt real. No Exit was something that could actually exist.

Bullying could become a punishable offense.

But is this the solution?

I don't know.

What do you think? Let me know.

And one last thing: Thank you. Thank you for, without knowing it, waiting six years to read this story.

Are you being bullied? Ask a teacher, your parents, or another family member for help.

Make sure to check out stopbullying.gov.

Do you have dark thoughts, or have you thought about suicide? Talk to someone about it! Call or text 988 and chat with someone there, or go to www.988lifeline.org.

You can also contact them if you're worried about someone else.

READ MORE FROM MAREN!